TO
DARE
A
Duchess

ISBN-13: 978-0-6484133-6-3
ISBN-10: 0-6484133-6-5

PROLOGUE

Edwina Granville, Duchess of Exeter, sat in a carriage on her way back to Granville Hall, a large and imposing estate that resembled a castle. With its impossibly high walls and turrets, and its location on top of a steep hill, the only architectural elements missing were towers and spiralling staircases. The building loomed over the town of Minehead, Kent and looked as superior as the duke she'd just married.

From this day on, now that their vows were spoken, this was her home. She looked back out the window and watched the church disappear from view, her parents still standing outside and greeting the few guests who had attended from London.

A rumbling snore sounded from beside her and she turned to see the Duke of Exeter asleep, his head lolling about and his mouth drooping as if he'd had a stroke. She sighed, having not thought this would be her husband at the end of her second Season, but here she was, a duchess and wife to a man who was old enough to be her grandfather.

Her stomach roiled at the idea of bedding him, but she would bear it, and she would tolerate it with a formidable strength, because that was her duty, what she'd been brought up to expect upon entering the marriage state. The carriage lurched as it started up the steep hill toward the Hall. Edwina, Nina to her friends, would play the obliging, attentive wife for one reason and one reason only.

Because anything was better than to be seen by the man she loved as a pitiful, sad gentlewoman who had lost her head with the worst outcome. She narrowed her eyes, fisting her hand in her lap as she recalled the reason she was in this predicament.

Mr. Andrew Hill, a gentleman who had made her believe she meant more to him than she truly did. A bastard and flirt if ever there was one, and a man whom she should've stayed the hell away from. But she did not, could not if she were honest with herself. And now she was married to a duke, would have his children and be an upstanding woman of rank whenever they travelled to town.

Nina supposed she should feel guilty marrying a man she did not love, but she could not. The leech beside her was only too willing to marry a woman so many years beneath him in age it ought to be illegal, but her money and her family made her too much of a temptation. So when he'd offered, in her desperation about being slighted, she'd said yes. The one saving grace, she supposed, was the fact that the duke already had a son. One who was older than herself, which made for awkward meetings, especially because his wife, the marchioness, hated Nina with more passion than she loved her husband.

Nina stared at the grey velvet upholstery seat across from her. The decision to marry the duke had been made

with such haste on her part, she hadn't considered in depth what it really meant for her.

Her time in London would now be curtailed somewhat, due to the fact the duke disliked town so much and left the entertaining to his son. A silver lining, perhaps, to the awful situation in which she now found herself. At least she wouldn't have to face the man who'd ruined all her dreams, and her in the process. Wouldn't have to face Society and their snickering snide looks because she'd sold herself into a loveless marriage and to a man twice her age.

The way she had fooled herself that she would be different from her parents, that she would have a grand love match when she took her vows, now mocked her to her core.

Nina sighed, staring down at her fingers. She would miss her friends, and one more than most. Byron, twin brother to Andrew, the blaggard who'd taken what he wanted with no iota of remorse. A man who could up and announce his engagement to someone other than herself could never really have cared for her. She would miss Byron though. He had left for the continent before her wedding and she wasn't sure when she'd see him again. She hoped it would be soon, but she wouldn't fool herself. She would probably never see him again.

CHAPTER
ONE

Kent. Five years later.

Nina sat on a blanket on the lawns behind Granville Hall and watched as Molly and Lora ran about chasing their wolfhound, Bentley, who was three times the children's size. The dog had been Molly and Lora's constant companion since the day they were born, and even though their grandmother worried and fretted about the young children being bitten, or worse, mauled by the large animal, Nina knew Bentley would never hurt them.

But she could not guarantee the dog wouldn't hurt others if he thought they were a threat.

Molly laughed, rolling onto the ground, and Nina chuckled when Bentley sat on Molly's back, holding her down. Lora tried to shift the dog off her sibling, to no avail.

"Mama, I'm stuck," her daughter yelled, her sweet little voice full of mirth.

She shrugged, shading her eyes to keep watch. "You

seem to have lost this war, Molly. Maybe a treat for Bentley since he's the victor I think."

The mention of the word *treat* had Bentley trotting over to her, and she clasped the wolfhound's face, kissing the bridge of his nose. "Off to Cook. Go see what Cook's made you."

Molly and Lora squealed their excitement and started for the back of the house, running as fast as their little legs would carry them, but not as fast as Bentley who'd already disappeared from view. Their cook Mrs. Jones would have an abundance of treats both for the dog and the children. Nina stood and shook out the blanket, ready to go indoors now that the sun was getting lower in the western sky.

How she would miss this estate. But it was time for her to return to town, take part in a Season and help pave the way for her children in the years to come. Not that she was looking for another husband—one had been plenty enough, and a loveless marriage was not an easy life to lead. And there was no reason why she should look for another man to warm her bed. She was wealthy in her own right, owned multiple homes, and was about to embark on a new direction here in her home county of Kent. Even so, as busy as she was with the planning of her village school, she missed her friends—in particular her cousin's wife, the Duchess of Athelby, whose letters had become more and more insistent she return to London.

And so she would, and for the first time since having the children she would leave them here in Kent. To do so had not been an easy choice, but with their studies, and her desire for them to breathe fresh country air instead of the coal-clogged air of London, it would be better this way. Of course she would return home at times throughout the Season to see them.

"Your Grace, an express has arrived from the Duchess of Athelby. It is on your desk in the library."

"Thank you, I'll be in directly."

The maid bobbed a curtsy and left her. Nina started for the terrace doors that led into the Hall's abundantly stocked library. The room was lined with mahogany wooden panels and book shelving. Books from all over the world stacked the walls from floor to ceiling. A pair of buttoned leather chairs sat strategically before a window, grabbing the light from the outdoors. A fire burned in the grate, warm and inviting. Going to her desk that sat in the center of the room, Nina picked up the missive and broke the ducal seal. She skimmed the note, clasping the desk for support as the safe little world she'd made for herself dissipated before her eyes.

Dearest Nina,

I feel I must warn you to prepare yourself for your return to town. Mr. Andrew Hill has returned from Ireland to have a London Season and is married, as you know. You must expect to see them both. I'm so sorry, dearest. I know this is not the news you would want from me. I shall see you in a few days.

Darcy.

NINA SCRUNCHED UP THE NOTE AND FOUGHT NOT TO CAST UP HER accounts. Andrew was back in town! Oh dear lord, no. Of all the Seasons she was to attend, he would have to choose this one as well. To see him again after so many years, to hear his voice, the sound of his laugh, the smell of his skin... However would she bear it? However would she remain civil and not slap his deceiving, lying face?

She remembered back to the night of her shame. The details were so clear it was almost as if it had happened yesterday. Having snuck into Andrew's room in the middle of the night, taking advantage of his inebriated state and seducing him wasn't the proudest moment of her life. But he'd been so caring, so loving toward her that evening, that she was sure he would offer for her. He had not. Instead the rogue had announced his betrothal the following morning to a Miss Fionna O'Connor, and had ripped her heart right out of her body.

Nina immediately acted like the silly youth she was at the time, and had given in to what her parents had always wanted for her—a grand match. And so within an hour of Andrew's announcement she was engaged to a duke and would move on from being the dutiful daughter to the dutiful wife.

A light knock sounded on the door and a footman entered, bowing before her. "Lunch is served, Your Grace."

"Have it brought in here, please. I have some correspondence to attend to that cannot wait. Also, send a note to the stables to have them prepare the carriages for my return to London three days from now. And send in my maid, please."

The footman bowed again. "Yes, Your Grace."

Nina walked over to the fire and sat on a leather wingback chair, staring at the flames licking the wood in the grate. Her decision to leave Molly and Lora behind was even more sensible than before. The girls had features that were so similar to Andrew's she was certain that if he ever got a glimpse of the children, he would know they were his. He was a proud man, or certainly was when she'd known him last, and he would not care for them being under another man's name when they ought to have his.

She clasped her hands in her lap to stop them from shaking. If she were to survive the Season, survive seeing the one man in the world whom she'd loved with such passion, with her whole heart, she would need to get a better hold of herself.

Andrew Hill broke her heart once. He would not have that power again.

The Season in town was not something Byron Hill thought he'd ever have to endure again. And yet here he was, back in London, fiancée in tow, and about to enjoy these last few months of the Season before he married Miss Sofia Custer.

She was not the type of woman that he'd ever thought to marry. Sofia was from a family of miners—hardworking, honest people who had enabled her every desire in life. The Custers owned practically all the copper mines there were in England, and as their only daughter Sofia enjoyed the luxuries that such a life brought her. She was a little immature, he supposed, and used to getting her own way, but they got along well enough and it was time he settled down to start a family of his own.

Byron stood out front of White's and kicked his heels waiting for Hunter, the Marquess of Aaron to arrive. The gentleman was already five minutes late and if he didn't arrive soon the footman standing out front of White's would move Byron on.

9

A hackney pulled to a stop and Hunter jumped down, coming toward him with a smile. "Byron, how good to see you again," he said, clasping his shoulder and shaking his hand.

Byron smiled back, delighted to see his cousin again too. "It's been a long time. Too long." And yet in a lot of ways, not long enough.

"Let us walk toward Hyde Park and catch up. The weather is congenial enough."

Byron couldn't agree more. The day had dawned warmer than normal for March, and after his long voyage back from the continent, a stroll sounded just the thing. "Tell me everything that has happened since I've been away."

Hunter laughed, his cane tapping a crescendo on the cobbled footpath. "I could ask the same of you. I hear you're to be married. I met Miss Custer two Seasons ago, before the family travelled abroad. She seemed very pleasant and intelligent. I'm assuming by the fact that Byron Hill, an eligible bachelor if ever there was one, is marrying you've found the love of your life?"

The bold question caught Byron off guard and he balked at the idea of answering his cousin. There wasn't any love between him and Sofia, even though they did get along very well. Byron hoped that in time perhaps their mutual like and respect would grow into deeper, meaningful emotions, but that would take time.

"It is not a love match, no. I leave those emotions to you and Cecilia." He ought to want more for Sofia, and himself, but to love someone again? No. He gave his heart away many years ago and had never really got it back.

The memory of Edwina Fox, now the Duchess of Exeter, a woman who only had eyes for his twin brother

Andrew, made his teeth ache. To this day the memory of them together, of watching them at balls and parties dancing and laughing at mutual jests, made Byron's blood boil. He pushed the recollection away, not wishing to feel melancholy when being back in town was a good thing. It was time for him to move on, marry and settle down.

His cousin had a whimsical look on his face before he said, "I'm not ashamed to say that I love my wife, adore her beyond what any respectable gentleman should, and I would not change my situation for the world. But are you sure you wish to partake in such a union? If there is no love, there is no guarantee that there ever will be, and to marry someone is a lifelong commitment. I do not want to see you make a mistake, Byron."

"I made my biggest mistake many years ago. This is merely a trifling matter." The declaration simply slipped out and he was unable to rip it back. "Apologies, Hunter, it seems London has many ghosts that want to come back and haunt me."

His cousin threw him an assessing look. "How is Andrew? I understand he returned from Ireland last week."

"He did, and Fionna accompanied him. They will be returning to Ireland after my marriage and the Season's end." They came to the corner of Upper Brook Street and Park Lane, and crossed the street before heading into Hyde Park. In the distance they could see a group of children running in the direction of the Serpentine. Women strolled and rode in carriages along with a few gentlemen who preferred horseback. The park was full of London society out for their daily dose of gossip and exercise.

They started along the Broad Walk both lost in thought for a time and content with silence. It was one of the things

Byron loved most about his cousin—they didn't always have to fill the silence with meaningless chatter.

"Now that you're back in England and Andrew resides in Ireland most of the time, have you taken over the London townhouse?"

Byron nodded, watching two boys run about as their nurse kept watch over them from under a large oak tree. "I have. I'll make it our home until we find something closer to Sofia's family in Cornwall." Which was a long way from London, and just as he liked it. He didn't wish to be anywhere near the city where he could run into Edwina at any given moment. Not that she was aware of his feelings—she'd only ever had eyes for his brother and never gave Byron a second glance.

"The townhouse will suit you very well, and with Andrew staying there for the Season at least, it'll give his wife and your future one time to acquaint themselves."

"Very true," he replied, having not given the situation much thought. As it was, Byron wasn't certain Sofia would get along very well with Andrew's wife. Fionna O'Connor came from titled stock in Ireland, and to have a future sister-in-law who hailed from mining stock wouldn't reflect as well on Fionna as she might like. He would have to ensure that she didn't put on any airs to cause offence to Sofia.

"I'm attending the Tattersalls auction on Thursday. Would you care to join me? With none of us living in England for some years now, we have no cattle. The mews is empty, save for the carriage that is stored there. I would like your opinion on a grey mare that I spied for Sofia, if you're available."

"I shall drop Cecilia off at her charity meeting and meet you there."

"Is Cecilia still very much occupied with the London Relief Society? Having children has not slowed her down?" Byron asked, smiling in fondness as he thought of the woman who had captured, and saved, his cousin. What a remarkable woman she was—always helping others, kind natured and loving. Hunter was a very lucky man indeed.

"I very much doubt anything will ever slow Cecilia down. She's simply marvellous. Speaking of marvellous things, the London Relief Society is holding a charity ball Saturday next. We're holding it at our home and would love for you to attend. Do you think you're free?"

And so it would begin, the whirl and madness of the Season. Even if this was only a charity ball, it was the start of many. But then it would be good for his fiancée to meet his extended family, and maybe Sofia would like to volunteer with the charity organization. "We would be honored to attend," he said sincerely.

Hunter chuckled, throwing him a bemused glance. "You may regret those words, cousin. A charity ball it may be, but bring your pocket book. Cecilia and the ladies who volunteer will be collecting donations and they'll not let you leave without some sort of monetary contribution."

Byron smiled. "Duly noted. I shall not forget." They started back toward the park gates. Would Nina be at this charity ball? Byron cursed his own longing at wanting to see her again, glimpse her from afar, while also praying that he wouldn't. He took a fortifying breath. He would have to be stalwart should he see her. One thing he never wanted Nina to know was how her marrying someone else had almost broken him in two. *Had* broken him in two, and he was still mending the fracture.

CHAPTER

TWO

With his fiancée on his arm, Byron walked up the steps to the London home of his cousin Hunter, the Marquess of Aaron, and waited in line to be received by their host and hostess for the evening.

The line was long, and already the charity ball was looking to be a crush. It would seem that Cecilia had fitted perfectly into the marquess's exalted status in society and made it her own. Just as she should, for Bryan had never met a kinder woman.

Meeting the marquess and marchioness, Byron introduced Sofia, and kissed Cecilia in welcome. His brother, who was standing behind him, did the same for Fionna and then they entered the ballroom. The large, rectangular room glowed with candlelight, and already some couples were dancing. Byron took in the room, having not expected the grandeur of the spectacle to cause a twinge of nostalgia to hit him. The last time he'd been in a ballroom he'd been a green lad, still wet behind the ears and eager to live life to the fullest in London, or at least that was how it seemed. In truth it had only been five or so years, but much had changed since he'd left. He wasn't the green, malleable man he once was. No longer did he allow others to dictate his life or tell him what to do, or how to act.

Andrew took Fionna out to dance and Byron turned to Sofia. "Shall we dance also, my dear?" he asked, glancing over her shoulder when a vision in red caught his eye. He stilled, his arm held out to take Sofia's, and the breath in his lungs seized.

Edwina Fox. Damnation, it was her.

Sofia nodded. "Thank you, yes."

Byron shut his mouth with a snap and schooled his features into an expression of indifference. For all that he and Edwina shared, she wasn't privy to the secret he carried, and never would be if he could help it. Only his cousin Hunter—who came across Byron the morning after Byron's error of judgement and demanded he tell him the truth—knew his secret. And he would keep it that way until he was dead.

Byron started toward the dance floor, but before he could take two steps, Edwina's attention strayed to where he stood and he read the moment she recognized him. Somehow, even though he was a twin, she'd almost always been able to tell him and Andrew apart. Maybe it was the single dimple on their cheeks, on opposite sides, but he wasn't smiling right now.

She started toward them, her beautiful, warm smile just for him. Or at least that was what he told himself before he reined in the idiocy that tended to come to the fore whenever he was around her.

"Byron," she said, coming up to him before leaning up and kissing his cheek. "I'm so glad you're here this Season. It has been too long since I saw you last."

The intoxicating scent of jasmine was like a physical blow to his gut. The years of not being near her—not being able to smell her sweet scent, hear her voice or view her beautiful face—almost felled him like an old oak in a storm.

He stared at her a moment, unable to do anything else. Christ, she was beautiful—her dark hair the color of the night sky, her perfect creamy complexion, and her laughing blue eyes. Not to mention the adorable dimples on her cheeks that he'd kissed and kissed again after their one night of sin.

"Your Grace, how lovely to see you again." His voice was formal, lifeless even, and Sofia stared up at him with a look of confusion on her face. He gestured to his fiancée. "Your grace, may I introduce Sofia Custer, my betrothed."

Edwina smiled as Sofia bobbed a small curtsy. "It's lovely to meet you, Miss Custer, and congratulations on your engagement. I had heard you were engaged and I'm glad to hear it is so. I'm very happy for you and Byron."

Byron swallowed the bile that rose in his throat at having Edwina so very close to him, and yet never had their distance been so far. "Is His Grace here this evening?" Asking after Edwina's husband made Byron want to snarl. He'd hated the curmudgeonly old slime who preyed on young women of fortune. Edwina was his latest victim.

Edwina frowned. "No, my stepson the Duke of Exeter is here. Maybe you have not heard, but my husband passed away some years ago now."

"I had not heard," he managed to stammer out, the room spinning. She was unmarried? A widow? "If you'll excuse us, Your Grace, I promised Sofia the next dance." He dragged his fiancée out onto the floor and lined them up with the other couples setting up for a quadrille.

"What an interesting and enlightening meeting that was," Sofia said, smiling across at him.

Byron didn't see anything at all amusing in what had just happened. If anything, never had he ever been in more pain. He thought he'd prepared himself to see her again, watch her dancing with her husband and enjoying the Season. He had not been prepared to see her unmarried.

"You think so?" he said, throwing himself into the dance with more zest than was necessary, hoping Sofia would change the subject.

"I do. You have friends in high places, Byron. I'm surprised you never mentioned before that your cousin is a marquess or that you are friends with a duchess."

Friends with a duchess. How he wished that were true. Of course it was in a way—they had once been the best of friends—but he'd wanted so much more than that. Since he and his brother Andrew were twins, with looks that replicated the other to perfection, he'd never understood why she'd gravitated toward Andrew and not him. Andrew was by far the more sedate and gentlemanly of the two of them, more willing to listen to and care for others. While Byron... well, he enjoyed life, the outdoors, and riding, and not just in regards to horses. He was the wild one, he supposed, and mayhap it was not what she was looking for at the time.

And now it was too late.

His fiancée linked arms with him, peering up at him. "I'm not blind, Byron. I saw the way you looked at her. You cared for the duchess once. Maybe even still do."

If there was one good thing about his understanding with Sofia Custer it was the promise they'd made each other to be always honest. No matter what that honesty may cost. But could he be truthful on this? He didn't wish to hurt her, but the laughing gaze she looked up at him with told him she wasn't the least piqued over his reaction to the duchess.

"I did care for her. Once. But that is long over now." He twirled her through one of the steps. "I'm willing to put the past behind me, be friends with the duchess. She seems amenable to the idea, and with her alliance, and that of my cousins, you'll have a good position here in Society. We will have friends who'll support us."

Sofia shrugged. "I care little for this Society. Once we're married, we'll travel back to Cornwall and you'll help father run the mines, just as we agreed."

"Of course," he said, bowing as the dance came to an end. "Shall we return to Hunter and Cecilia? I'm sure they would love to catch up with you some more and get to know you better."

Again Sophia shrugged, seemingly little interested in his family.

Was she angry at him? Was she jealous after all regarding Edwina? He supposed there was a chance that she liked him more than they had admitted to, but then they'd had so little time together he really didn't think that was possible. You couldn't be jealous of someone you hardly knew and who hardly knew you in return. When they'd met abroad in Rome, while Sofia was visiting the continent with her family, they'd enjoyed each other's company. He'd taken them to the sights of Paris, of Rome and Florence. They had always had something to talk about, but having returned to London, that carefree life had ended and with it their conversation had dried up. He'd proposed to Sofia after a wonderful day boating off the coast of southern France and it had seemed the perfect end to a perfect day. He was of an age where he longed for a family of his own, to have a wife and not a mistress, and

Sofia suited that role very well. But upon returning to England and the realities that came with that—his town life and her Cornwall one—their compatibility wasn't as good as he thought.

When they returned to his cousin, Cecilia greeted Sofia warmly and asked if she would like to join her for a turn about the room. A sliver of relief shot through Byron when the ladies walked off into the throng of guests. That in itself was telling of the emotional bond between them, which was very little.

"You are as pale as a ghost, cousin. Is your cravat too tight, or is your dear fiancée not too pleased with how you reacted when you saw Edwina Fox?" Hunter threw him a bemused glance, and Byron cringed.

"You saw that, did you? I'd hoped to mask my features before she noticed, but alas it seems I was unsuccessful."

Hunter took two glasses of whiskey from a passing footman and handed one to Byron.

"I have not forgotten what she meant to you. Edwina, I mean. It's been many years since you've seen her—it is any wonder that you reacted so? I'm sure it was like seeing a ghost. But remember, cousin, Nina doesn't know it was you in that room that night and so you need to be careful around her. Your mannerisms will give you away and she will start to wonder why it is that you act so strangely around her person."

Byron conceded Hunter's point. The memory of that night was so vivid in his mind it could've happened only yesterday, not five years ago.

The night of the Duke and Duchess of Athelby's annual ball, that was held that year at their country estate, had started like all of the events Byron had suffered through. Edwina Fox, as she was known then, had been enjoying her second Season in town, being courted by many, but had somehow managed to be known as cunning and cold, certainly when it came to her admirers. All her admirers but one—Byron's brother Andrew.

During her first Season she'd managed to slip the snare of Lord Wakely, who'd been rumored to marry her, but then he'd up and married Lizzie Doherty and so Edwina was free to do as she pleased.

His brother had always been sweet, polite and kind to the opposite sex, and Nina, like all the debutantes he'd ever met, loved to be admired and cherished. Byron knew the game his brother was playing—make many fall, play the admired gentleman the matrons of the ton adored, all the while courting someone out of the London elite set.

On the night of the ball and the day after his sibling had arrived at the estate, Andrew had come to him with a request. "Brother, I'm happy to have caught you before dinner. Would you mind if we swapped rooms this evening? The bed in my room is too hard, and I know you don't mind mattresses to be so, so I was hoping to swap."

Byron had rolled his eyes at his brother's problem. Typical of him to complain of the littlest troubles in life. "We're here one more night. Can you not put up with it?"

Andrew made a show of rubbing his back, and Byron should have guessed then, at his brother's terrible acting skills, that he was up to no good. "Please, Byron. I'll talk to our valets and have them move all our things. I cannot bear another night on that bed."

Byron cursed under his breath. "You've only slept on it one time as it is. Surely it's not too much of a hardship."

"I get no rest in it. You don't mind hard mattresses, please swap," his brother begged. "My back is already troubling me and it's only been one night, as you said."

"Fine," Byron said, not wanting to be bothered by such a petty problem. "Instruct your valet to change our rooms."

Andrew smiled, his relief evident. "Thank you, brother. I'll direct Walter to pack up both our things."

"You do that, and soon. I'm tired after my journey here today and a hard mattress or not, I'm looking forward to going to bed tonight."

CHAPTER
THREE

Byron stood at the base of his bed, staring at the vision that was Edwina Fox who'd entered his room not a moment before, shutting the door quickly behind her. Clad only in a dressing gown with a shift beneath, the cotton was so sheer that Byron could see the outline of her person in the light from the fire burning in the grate.

Holy bollocks, what is she doing here?

He'd headed to bed early after being the last to arrive for the Athelby ball held that very evening, taking a bottle of the duke's best whisky to his room to help him sleep. Just as his brother had informed him, the bed was terribly hard, so the liquor should help somewhat.

Nina snapped the lock on the door closed and he swallowed, blinking to clear his blurred vision. This was not what was supposed to happen. Nina loved his brother, not him. Had she had a change of heart? Had she finally seen his worth? He drank in the vision that was her, her hair cascading down her back, her long dark locks curling a little around her angelic face.

Hell, she was pretty. So beautiful and sweet. And damn it all to hell, he wanted her. Had wanted her to be his for so long, and here she was, finally after all the years they had been friends.

"Hello there, are you surprised to see me?" she asked, taking a step toward him.

Byron stepped back, the edge of the bed hitting his knees. "Yes. Yes, I am," he stuttered, shaking his head. "Edwina, you should leave. You being here is a mistake and one I do not wish for you to regret."

She closed the space between them and he had nowhere to go, unless he flopped back onto the bed. As she came toward him he fought not to notice how the light of the fire outlined her long, slim legs and the curvature of her waist.

She looked up at him uncertainly. "Don't send me away," she beseeched him. "You know I want you. We've been friends for so long, I have known you for an age. I want to kiss you. Let me."

Kiss her? Dear God, yes.

She leaned up, trying to capture his lips, and he clasped her shoulders and pushed her away. "Listen, Nina, are you sure? There is no turning back from this. One taste of you and I'll want you forever."

She shook her head, her dark locks bouncing with the effort. "I'm sure. Please kiss me and make me yours."

Byron debated with his own moral code. She was a maid, but then she was only asking for a kiss. What was the harm in that? He stared down at her, reading the longing in her stormy blue eyes, and his resolve to deny her crumbled.

Her hand slid against his bare chest, and he cursed the fact he'd stripped off his shirt after partaking in too much drink. Her touch seared his skin and left him burning wherever her palm moved. The room spun a little and he clasped the bed for support.

"Just a kiss and I'll sneak back to my room. No one ever needs to know."

Byron shut his eyes for a moment, not wanting to look at her, for he knew that if he did, he would crumble and do what she wished. Her beguiling tore him in two, and the years of denial, of always being on the sidelines, never the one that she wanted, rose to the surface and crashed all his defences. He could not deny her anything. Not even a kiss.

He caught her gaze. "I will kiss you. But only one."

She nodded, her eyes brightening with awareness and expectation. The smell of jasmine wafted from her hair and he shut his eyes, reveling in the essence of her.

Just before they kissed he took in her features. She had the most beautiful, perfectly arched brows. Lips that begged to be kissed, so plump with the slightest rosy hue. Her eyes were closed, her lashes perfect arcs against her cheeks. He placed a small kiss upon her nose, another on a cheek, and then kissed down to her chin, working his way around her jaw, wanting to savor the moment and not rush his time with her. The one and only kiss he would have with Nina.

She sighed, the whisper of her breath making his blood pump hard in his veins, and he took her mouth in a searing kiss. Her hands reached about his neck, holding him against her. Her breasts pushed upon his chest and he swore he could feel her heart pumping as fast as his own. The fluttering of her tongue touched his and his control snapped. He hoisted her against his hardened sex, desperate for her and unable to deny the feel of her lithe body in his arms.

He ground her against him and she moaned, a deep

seductive tone that he wanted to hear again and again. She undulated in turn, seeking her own pleasure, although she would not know just how it could be between a man and woman, not yet at least.

"Take me. Make me yours. I want you."

He tumbled them onto the bed. His hands without thought fought with her shift, wiggling it up her body to pool at her waist. She wore nothing beneath, and he swore. He wanted to kiss her mons that glistened in the firelight. Hear her moan his name. Make her climax under the touch of his lips. He wanted to do everything with her. One night would never be enough.

A little voice warned him against this course. It was wrong, what he was enticing her into. Edwina was a virgin. This action could ruin her chances of a good match, but the idea of her being with anyone else pushed away his guilt. He wanted her to be his, had been patient waiting for her to notice him. And now she had. He could no sooner push her away than he could push the sun away from the day.

He kissed her again and she sighed as he settled between her legs.

"Oh, Nina, you have no idea how much I want you. I've wanted you for so long it hurts."

Her fingers slid into his hair, pulling him down for another kiss. Her wish was his command—in her arms he would do anything she wanted, give her every desire if only she'd let him.

She lifted her legs, locking them about his hips. He took his cock in hand and guided himself into her hot, wet core. Blast she felt good, tight and warm and so deliciously wet. He gasped as he sheathed himself fully, her sharp intake of air holding him still a moment as he allowed her to familiarize herself with their joining.

"Are you well, Nina? I'm sorry I hurt you," he said, kissing the lobe of her ear. She relaxed in his hold and he fought not to continue. He wanted her with a desperation that could make him careless, and he didn't want that for her. He wanted her to remember this night forever. Wanted to be all that she desired and more. To be the beginning of them.

She clasped his face with her hands and met his gaze. "Don't stop." She nodded. "This is what I want."

And it had been what he'd wanted from that night on, right up to now as he watched Edwina, now the dowager Duchess of Exeter, talk with a group of ladies beside the ballroom floor. But fate the following morning had played its joker and he'd lost the game.

His brother came up beside him, joining in his conversation with Hunter.

"I must admit I'm pleased to be back in town," Andrew said, pulling Fionna closer to his side. "We should return more often, my dear. I'd forgotten how fun London could be."

She agreed amicably, and Byron fought not to roll his eyes at the banal chitchat his brother had with his spouse. Since their marriage five years earlier, his brother had become the most boring man on earth. Not that he hadn't been before. Really, Byron still could not understand the attraction that the women of the ton had for him.

"I saw you talking to the duchess. Is Edwina well?" Andrew asked, meeting Byron's eye.

"Very well, I can gather. She too is here for the Season," Byron said, trying to keep his composure when around the one woman who could discombobulate him at any given moment. He rubbed a hand over his jaw, his attention snapping back to the duchess. She cast a glance in their direction, and excusing herself from the group she stood with, started toward them.

Hunter cleared his throat, and Byron reminded himself that she did not know the truth. Didn't know it was him in her bed that night, not his brother. Unfortunately he had only found out that was who she'd thought he was after they had slept together. After walking Nina to his door and checking that the passage was vacant of guests he'd wished her goodnight, only to hear his brother's name whispered against his ear. Having his heart torn from his chest would've been less painful. He knew in that moment what a colossal mistake she had made, and he as well. That a night where he'd thought of nothing but beginnings would be only the end should Nina know the truth. Not that it mattered, for the following day both Nina and Andrew had made their choices and he was left with nothing.

Byron looked to his brother and didn't miss the flicker of fear that entered his sibling's eyes. He ought to be afraid too. Hell, they both should be if Nina were ever to find out the truth. The whole truth, some of which even Byron would never forgive himself for.

NINA CAME TO STAND BEFORE THE TWO BROTHERS, MARVELLING AT how similar they both were, identical in fact, and yet the years had not been kind to Andrew. He'd rounded in the five years since she'd seen him last. Whereas Byron had aged well, like a fine wine just ripe for the picking.

Nina checked herself. Such thoughts were not appropriate, and Byron was her friend. To have such a visceral reaction to him was not what duchesses did, no matter how much she wondered what lay beneath his superfine coat and perfectly starched waistcoat and shirt.

The men bowed and Andrew's wife made her a pretty curtsy, one that she didn't return. They didn't deserve such respect, or at least her husband did not.

"Duchess, how very well you look," Andrew said. "It has been many years."

The reminder of what they had done together prior to the years passing them by shot a blast of annoyance through her blood and she fought not to throw her glass of champagne over his head.

Not that she desired him in any way anymore. His treatment of her had put paid to such sentiments, but still, that did not mean she would allow him to enjoy his Season without a little payback.

"Some may say not long enough." An uncomfortable silence ensued and Nina smiled up at Byron. She'd started to wonder what it was exactly that she'd liked about Andrew in the first place. For a man to treat a debutante in such a deplorable manner, in light of what they'd done, made him no man she wanted to be associated with. "Are you here for the Season staying at your townhouse?"

"We are, Your Grace," Fionna said, smiling a little. "We hope to hold our own ball a little into the Season."

Nina had to concede that Andrew's wife was pretty, even though the last time she'd seen her, she'd been almost sick at the news of her engagement to the man who'd deflowered her the night before.

"How very lovely. I'm sure it'll be a great success."

"Please allow us to offer our condolences on the passing of the duke. His son has inherited the title I presume?" Andrew asked, his tone that of disinterest, which was exactly what Nina was feeling right at this moment.

"Matthew has inherited the title, and he and his wife are also in town this Season, although they spend most of their time at the estate in Derbyshire."

Byron frowned. "I thought the duke's home was in Kent."

"It was," Nina said, "but that home wasn't entailed and George left it to me, so it's where I live. I also have a townhouse on Berkley Square all to myself, which is one small comfort." Considering she'd married the duke without an ounce of attachment and that she'd then allowed him to believe the children she gave birth to were his.

"How are the girls?" Lord Aaron asked. "I understand they're staying in Kent while you're in London."

Nina had decided that, but when the time had come to part she couldn't leave them behind and so she'd bundled them up and brought them with her. "I was going to leave them in Kent, but decided against it. They're in London with me, and enjoying all the museums and parks that we don't get at home."

"You're a mother?"

The blunt question that came from Byron wasn't what Nina expected and she glanced at both brothers, hoping they would not pry too much into her life. Andrew certainly had no claim on her anymore, or her children, even if he was the father.

"I am—two girls, and my sole reason for living. They are simply my heart."

"How old?" Byron asked, his voice hoarse.

Nina wasn't willing to tell them anything further and she smiled in welcome as Cecilia, Lady Aaron joined them. Nina kissed her cheeks in welcome.

"How lovely to see you again, Cecilia. I've been meaning

to write, and I hope Darcy has maybe told you what I wish to do."

Cecilia nodded, going to her husband and linking arms with him. "She has, and I think it is the most marvellous idea."

"What is the idea?" Lord Aaron asked, throwing a curious glance at his wife.

"The duchess has purchased a vacant building in the village near her estate and she's going to make it into a school, and, for the children who require it, a place to live. We have two other schools based in the country, but this is our first in Kent. I'm so very excited about it."

Byron's betrothed joined them. Her long golden locks that sat high atop her head made her appear older than she was and her white muslin gown had a pretty pink ribbon at the waist. Coming up to Byron, she wrapped her hand about his arm. The familiarity between the two twisted something within Nina and for a moment she simply stared at where they were joined.

Miss Custer dipped into a curtsy, but her inspection of Nina seemed less than enthralled. "It's lovely to see you again, Your Grace," she said banally. "What is it that everyone is talking about?"

Cecilia caught Miss Custer up on their discussion about the new school, but even with this subject Byron's betrothed looked less than interested.

"I think it's just what is needed if we're to fight the divide between the classes," Nina added. "It is very hard to better oneself, but this new school will enable girls and boys to become whatever they wish, if they have the determination to do so."

Miss Custer scoffed. "I shall not be offering to put one up in Cornwall. We would lose half our workforce in the mines in a day should we do so. We rely on the youngins working for us." Sofia chuckled at her own statement, as if the poor and needy were something that one ought to find funny.

Nina fisted her hands at her side. "You believe that allowing children to work underground, inhaling air that is no good for their lungs, stopping them from possibly doing other employment that would certainly give them a longer, more satisfying life, is a bad thing?"

"I do," Sofia said, meeting her gaze. "Someone has to do the job and the children are most capable. I think your idea, no matter how revolutionary, will never happen."

A shiver stole down Nina's back at the coldness she read in the woman's eyes. No matter what Sofia said or what Nina did, they would never be friends. The dislike oozing from the woman towards her was palatable. Not to mention anyone who thought it proper to allow children to work in mines was no friend of hers.

"I disagree, Miss Custer, and I hope to see the end of children working in your family's mines. Children deserve so much more than what we, our society at large I mean, give them."

Sofia took a sip of her wine but didn't say anything further.

Their set fell into awkward silence and Nina couldn't help but narrow her eyes at the little Cornish chit. She especially wanted to say more to Miss Custer about her atrocious beliefs, but she did not. She was Byron's betrothed, and Byron was her friend. She would not embarrass him no matter how much she detested his future wife.

Fortunately Nina was then asked to dance by the Duke of Athelby and the night progressed well, save for the little hiccup with Miss Custer and her archaic views. She suppered with Darcy and discussed the plans for her new school, making her wish the Season was coming to an end, not just beginning, so she could go home and start the building work on her new property.

Byron came to sit with them during the repast. Darcy excused herself and Nina turned toward her old friend, glad to have some time alone with him.

She touched his arm lightly. "Have I told you how very happy I am that you're back in England? I thought for a time that you would never return."

He nodded slowly in agreement. "The draw of the sunshine simply was too much to deny."

Nina laughed, a sound she'd not heard often these past years, unless she was with her children of course, who always made her happy. "Come, Byron, even I know your words reek with sarcasm." She took in his features, his strong jaw and straight nose. Dark brown orbs the color of cocoa. How was it that she'd never looked at him with anything other than friendship? He was certainly hand-some, just as handsome as his brother once was, but maybe a little more wild. Was that the reason? Andrew had always seemed responsible, careful, and trustworthy. How wrong she'd been. All the time she'd been holding onto Andrew, placing him on a pedestal, hoping their union would be a love match, he'd been looking at someone else.

"I glad we're alone, Byron, because there is something that I want to discuss with you."

"You can tell me anything. What is it, Nina?"

His use of her name warmed her from the inside out. "The history between your brother and I...I do not want it to come between our friendship. You've always been there for me. My friend and rock. I have missed you these five years."

"I missed you too." He cleared his throat and took a sip of his wine. "Nothing will come between us. I will fight for our friendship no matter what obstacles we face. I promise you that."

"Well, let us hope there are no more obstacles and that we can move forward. I knew seeing Andrew with his wife would be difficult at first, but now after seeing him again, viewing him without the haze of adolescent idiocy, I simply cannot understand what I liked about him. He's a little vapid, don't you think?"

"Too true," Byron said, his eyes alight with mischief. "To be honest I could never understand what you saw in my brother either. And I love him, I do, but I never thought his character suited yours. I know you were known as a little cold and aloof during your first Season, but to me you've always been warm, funny, all too willing to laugh. I always thought you should marry a man who tested you, loved you wildly, and honored you. Andrew was never that."

The breath in Nina's lungs seized and she found herself entranced by Byron's eyes. How well he knew her, behind the façade she once hid behind. How had it been that he saw all that she was and could offer and Andrew had not? She sighed, supposing when one was looking at marrying someone else, their attention wasn't as focused as one thought.

A fluttering settled in her belly and she looked down at her champagne glass. Why was she reacting to Byron in such a way? For one, he was betrothed, and second, she was not looking for anyone to marry. Especially not one of the Hill brothers. No matter how much she loved her friend, she would not walk that road again. For the first time in years she was happy with who she was, a mother. The girls needed her and would need her guidance even more as they grew into young women. Being independently wealthy with her own estates afforded her a freedom most women could only dream of, and she wasn't willing to give that up, especially not to another man.

"I hope I have not offended you, Nina, with what I said."

She shook her head, smiling to put him at ease. "Of course not. I think what you said was lovely and I thank you. I know we'll always be friends, and I wanted to ensure that stayed so. As for me and your brother, well, we will never be friends again."

Nina read the understanding in her friend's eyes and she was thankful he was back in town. They used to have so much fun together, and with Byron back her Season would have another element of joy.

"I can understand your stance regarding my sibling, and I know there is no point in trying to change your mind. So," he said, holding out his hand, "shall we dance instead?"

She slid her gloved fingers into his hold, grinning. "I would love to."

CHAPTER
FOUR

Byron strolled into the breakfast room the following morning and was glad to find Andrew there alone. He served himself up a couple of veal and ham pies, along with poached eggs and a piece of toast, before sitting. A footman poured him a coffee and Byron took a moment to gather his thoughts.

Andrew folded the newspaper he was reading and placed it beside him on the table, dismissing the servants from the room. Byron glared at him across the mahogany space and Andrew looked at him in surprise, no doubt wondering what had put his mood out of sorts.

"The night that you told me to stay in your room at the Athelby's country estate, due to your hard mattress if you recall, tell me that Nina turning up was not orchestrated by you," Byron said, watching his sibling. "Tell me that you did not know she was going to enter your room and offer herself like a sweetmeat on a plate."

Andrew's eyes widened and Byron knew his summarisation of his brother had been correct. He had set him up! Had known that Nina was coming to his room, and had deposited Byron there to face her instead. Made Byron believe she had been there for him, while all the time she was there for his brother. "You bastard, Andrew. I ought to get up right now and pummel you to a pulp."

Andrew placed his coffee down with enough force for the liquid to spill a little onto the white tablecloth. "What if I did know? It is too late to change things now. I wanted to marry Fionna and Edwina stood in the way of that." His brother shrugged and a red haze closed over Byron's vision. "I was surprised by her blatant dislike for me last evening–it was more than I expected from a woman who'd simply been told that I wouldn't marry her. She seemed scorned to me."

"That's because she was scorned. Scorned by you. The following morning she arrived downstairs to find you announcing your betrothal to Miss O'Connor. What did you expect from Nina? Joy? Congratulations? You do not deserve anything from her."

Andrew studied him a moment and Byron fought to keep his hands unclenched. The silence was long, and when he met his brother's hardened gaze he knew Andrew had figured out his secret. "You slept with her, didn't you? She arrived at my room, thinking it was me, and you took advantage of that. She thinks I slept with her the night before I announced my engagement to Fionna."

Andrew ran a hand through his hair and for a moment Byron's calm and patience cracked a little. "I thought she was there for me. How did you know she was going to come to your room?"

His brother shifted on his seat, adjusting his cravat. "She sent me a missive that day, saying she wanted to talk in private. I could not meet with her, obviously, and I suppose I panicked. The bed was hard, I will admit Byron, and so us swapping rooms was necessary for me to sleep, but I did not think she would follow through on her plan. I seem to have been wrong."

"You were bloody well wrong alright. She thinks you slept with her the night before your betrothal. She doesn't know it was me. This can all be laid at your door, you damn fool. Why would you not just send her a note stating your affections lay elsewhere? Do you have no conscience?" His brother was a coward and damn it to hell, how would Byron ever gain Nina's forgiveness over this mess.

"I cannot have my wife hearing that I supposedly deflowered a virgin before asking for her hand. Fionna would never forgive me," Andrew said, standing and letting his chair fall back against the floor.

Anger thrummed through Byron's veins and he fought not to lose his temper. "I swapped rooms to allow you to sleep. I did not know she was going to arrive at my door and ask for things you damn well know I'd longed to hear from her for years. You played me and Nina to gain your own happy ever after."

"And during all the time she was in your room, can you honestly say that a name wasn't uttered? Did you not wonder at it, Byron?"

Byron swallowed the bile that rose in his throat. He had not wondered. Being so caught up in the delight of having her in his arms had made him incapable of clear thought. He'd truly believed she was there for him. What a fool he'd been. And the moment she'd whispered his brother's name just as she left, a little piece of him had died.

"I did not think my blood could use me in such a way. I will not be fooled twice, brother." Byron stood, taking a calming breath. "I must tell her the truth of it."

Andrew gestured with his arms, knocking over the

remainder of his coffee. "Of course you need to tell her. Edwina woke the following morning and watched me announce my engagement to everyone at the house party, all the while thinking we'd made the beast with two backs the night before."

Byron stormed over to his brother, ready to rip his damn head off. His sibling stumbled back and fell over his chair, landing with a loud thump on his ass. "If your precious Fionna finds out how you used Nina, courted her and flirted with her during her two Seasons, then you deserve her wrath. Tricking your own brother to save your own hide, well, you have lost any respect I once held for you. I will allow you to stay here for the remainder of the Season and then you shall return to Ireland and stay there. You do not deserve me as a brother, or Nina as a friend."

"Who do you think you are?" Andrew yelled, pointing a finger at him. "You could've offered for her. Why did you not make an honest woman of your precious Nina? Instead, you allowed her to marry a man old enough to be her grandfather."

Byron clenched his fists. "You damn well know I came downstairs only to find both of you engaged and basking in the grand matches you'd made. I couldn't say anything to Nina. She would've been ruined, and as much as she loved me as a friend, she was infatuated with you. It would've broken her heart, and she'd already had that broken seeing you engaged to Fionna. I could not break it twice in one day."

How he'd wanted to go to her that morning. To take her in his arms and tell her to marry him instead. That he would make her happy, keep her safe, and give her all that she wanted in life. A part of him had been a coward, scared to lose her even as a friend should he tell her the truth, but no longer. He would tell her now, and be damned the consequences. And he would tell her soon.

Andrew stood, dusting down his buckskin breeches. "I will accept my part in this sorry mess, but now you must tell her the truth. I'll not have her believing it was me who took her maidenhead."

Byron thought over how he would even begin to tell Nina. When she knew the truth of that night she'd never speak to him again, and the idea of the severing from a woman who had always been his friend, a woman whom he'd fallen in love with that Season all those years ago, made him want to retch. He swallowed. "Of course I'll tell her the truth. But this isn't something that you can just blurt out to anyone at any time. I wronged her. You wronged her. And this will devastate her."

Andrew snatched the paper from the table and started toward the door. "It needs to be done, and soon. I'll give you the time you want, but don't drag it out simply because it'll be hard for her to hear."

Byron watched his brother leave, resisting the urge to throw a plate at his head. Andrew had always been a heartless prig, only worrying about his own hide in any situation. In the five years since Byron had seen him last, his sibling had not changed one bit for the better.

Byron sighed, righting his brother's chair and looking over the mess of the breakfast table. He sat back down before his now cold meal. He picked up his fork as his mind turned to what he would have to do, and how Nina would handle hearing the truth. No matter how much he'd loved her, how much he'd longed for her, it was not him she'd wanted. He should've known the night she came to his room that she was mistaken, that they were both under miscomprehensions.

The cost of that night would be greater than he'd ever imagined, and possibly too much for a friendship to recover from.

Nina stood on the steps before the Hill brothers' London home. Not a location she'd thought she'd ever grace again, and yet here she was. She rapped on the door using the iron knocker. She looked out onto the square and smiled at a couple of passers-by before the door opened and a footman greeted her.

"Mr. Byron Hill, please." She handed him her card. "Tell him the Dowager Duchess of Exeter is here to see him."

The footman bowed, stumbling over his words to grant her entrance and do as she asked, before he disappeared into one of the rooms leading off the foyer.

The quickened steps on parquetry floor sounded before Byron came out of a room, smiling in welcome.

"Your Grace, how wonderful to see you again. I hope everything is well."

Nina smiled at her old friend, again so very pleased he was back in town. "Everything is well, but I was hoping you would accompany me today. I'm purchasing the desks that are required for the school I'm opening in Kent, and I'd like your opinion on them."

He threw her a dubious look. "Are you sure you wish me to accompany you? The Duchess of Athelby or Marchioness of Aaron may be better suited, since they already run two schools here in town."

She clasped her hands before her and fought to ignore the fact her pulse quickened at the sight of him. Why was it now that she found her dearest friend so very alluring? Was it simply because he was betrothed and therefore not a suitor she could have? Or the fact that she'd loved him as a friend for years and was only now seeing him for his worth?

It could also be both...

"Darcy and Katherine have given me the name and address of their supplier and he's expecting me, but I'd like the company. Men, as you know, sometimes find it hard to be fair when dealing with women."

Byron called for his coat and cane and took them from the footman when they were fetched. "I would love to join you, of course. I just assumed a duchess would have servants who would do such tasks."

"I do have them, but it's something I want to do. I may be a duchess, but that doesn't mean I sit at home lording it over everyone else. How boring my life would be if that were the case."

"And let's not forget you're a mother now, something I simply cannot imagine. You must let me meet your daughters. I'd so love to get to know them."

"I'd love that too. We'll have to ensure you meet before you head to Cornwall. Living in that faraway county, we'll never see you." And if lady luck were on her side, Byron wouldn't recognize the fact the girls looked nothing like her husband but someone else entirely.

He stared at her for a moment before clearing his throat and gesturing toward the door. "Shall we?"

They made their way to her carriage, which sat parked at the front of the townhouse. Byron took her hand, helping her up the step. The feel of his strong touch, even through her kid-leather gloves, left her mind reeling. She would have to get hold of her emotions, of her reactions to him. Acting like a lovesick ninny would never do, especially now that he was engaged to another.

"The location is not too far. Thank you for coming. It gives us more time to catch up." She settled onto the squabs, aware that her carriage was probably a lot grander than what Byron had, but other than looking about the equipage with delight, he didn't comment on the opulence.

"How many desks are we purchasing today?" he asked.

Nina was glad the conversation had diverted in a practical direction—it saved her from asking him what he loved about Sofia Custer. After their conversation last evening, Nina couldn't find a lot to like in the woman who agreed with child labour.

"One hundred. I've seen some desks that have a little lid on them that opens and allows the children to keep their chalkboards or lunch beneath it. It's most revolutionary and the design I'm most interested in."

"A hundred desks will cost you."

Nina barked out a laugh. The cost was the least of her problems. "I'm an extremely wealthy woman, Byron. You needn't worry I'm spending my pin money."

His cheeks reddened and he leaned forward, taking her hand from her lap. "Apologies, Duchess. That was very crass of me. In fact, I don't know why I mentioned it. I suppose out of concern and friendship."

Nina squeezed his hand then broke the contact. Why was it now that he discombobulated her so? He never used to. "Where did you go after the Athelby house party where we saw each other last? Your brother hightailed it to Ireland and he never gave me a forwarding address for you. I wanted to write, tell you everything that had happened, but I didn't know where to send the missives."

He glanced out the window, the muscle on his temple working. "That day, that we parted, I'd prefer to forget. I slept late and came down to a house in uproar, or at least in jubilation uproar. My brother engaged to Miss O'Connor and you engaged to the Duke of Exeter. I thought I was living in an alternate universe."

Nina had often felt the same. Her hasty decision to accept the duke after hearing the news of Andrew's engagement had been financially rewarding, and the duke, no matter how much older than herself, had not been unkind. But if she had her time again she would not have done it. She would've ruined herself, publicly declared that Andrew had deflowered her, and demanded he marry her. Not that their marriage would've been any good under such beginnings, but the fact that he could do such a thing to her and then marry someone else still irked. How could anyone be so heartless?

"I will not insult you by declaring that I loved the duke and didn't want another, for you know that would be a lie. I married the duke because Andrew broke my heart, foolish and young as it was then, but nevertheless he did, and I wanted to prove to him that he was not the only one who could be so unfeeling, so cold and aloof. I suppose I really did live up to how people viewed me after all."

"I'm sorry about my brother and his actions toward you."

Nina scoffed. What would Byron think if he knew the whole truth? That Andrew hadn't just broken her heart, but had ruined her. Looking back, she knew she'd been fortunate that the duke had asked for her hand. Had he not, she would've had to tell her parents that she was with child once she realized the truth herself, and that the father was a married man. Such news would not have been welcomed by her parents or by society at large.

"Not as sorry as I am that I fell for his pretty words, but," she said, wanting to end this discussion, "let us discuss my new venture and the Season ahead of us." She didn't want to spend a moment more thinking about Andrew Hill or his treachery. She wanted to look to her and her children's future, the future for all the children she'd help with her school in Kent.

Byron's lips lifted into a small smile. "I heartily agree. Now, tell me where exactly this school is going to be. I'll need to know so when I get back to town I can order and send books down to you. A school is nothing without a library."

Warmth spread through Nina and she felt an over-whelming urge to hug him. "Your generosity will not be forgotten. Thank you, Byron. You're too good."

He threw her a wicked grin, and for the life of her she could not look away. The pit of her stomach clenched and the carriage suddenly seemed awfully small and confined.

Byron cleared his throat, and she was glad of the distraction. "Have you been a member of the London Relief Society for long? How did you become involved?" he asked, the tension of the moment relieved by his genuine interest in her work.

"The Duke of Athelby is a relative, and I knew Darcy was involved for some years. My husband didn't like coming to town much, so I would often visit the small village at the base of our home in Kent. Even in a quiet village I could see that there were children without school-ing, children without proper care or food. I want to change that. Help where I can."

"You always did have a heart of gold. Your daughters must be very proud of you."

Nina smiled thinking of her girls. "I hope they are, or they will be at least when they're older. I want them to be strong and kind women. Women of power who want to make a difference in the lives of others."

"You'll be wanting the vote next," Byron said, grinning at her.

Nina sighed. He'd been her friend for so many years, and they had always got along so well. To be around him for more than snippets of time would be no hardship. It was certainly something she would enjoy on a daily basis if she could. "I hope one day that we do have the right. It is only fair and just that women have what men have, and have the same opportunities as well. I want that for my girls and I'll not apologize for my opinions."

"I wouldn't want you to," he whispered, meeting her gaze.

She chuckled to hide the rioting emotions he seemed to conjure in her. "I'm glad you're back in London. Thank you for coming on my jaunt today."

"What are friends for if not to help each other?"

Friends... The word echoed through her mind. Did she want to only be friends with Byron? She studied him as he looked out the window at the passing streets of London. Her attention travelled over his attire. His suede buckskin breeches required no padding on his muscular thighs. His shoulders were broad and his black greatcoat only made him look larger, more dangerous and brawny. They had always been the best of friends, but now, seeing him with Miss Custer, she wasn't so sure she liked the idea that he was destined for another. Didn't want to imagine him beside his wife in the privacy of their room, his body hers to enjoy, to run her hands over and play with. Miss Custer's and Miss Custer's alone.

Just as Nina had made a mistake with Andrew, she now realized she'd also made a terrible error of judgement with

Byron. But what to do about that error? Not since her youthful folly with Andrew had she felt this desire to be with a man, but she was certainly feeling it now with Byron. Should she dissuade him from marrying Miss Custer? Or should she acknowledge the fact that they were only ever meant to be friends and nothing more?

Surely if they were meant to be together fate would've stepped in years ago and showed its hand. It had not. Even so, Nina debated with herself over what she wanted and what was right, and at this very moment in time, the selfish part of her wanted Byron for herself and Miss Custer could go hang.

CHAPTER FIVE

Two nights later Nina attended the Duke and Duchess of Athelby's annual ball. Their London home was one of the capital's finest, and just as the house was magnificent, so too was the decoration and floral arrangements that Darcy loved to have throughout the ballroom.

Entering the room, one would've thought they had stepped into a forest landscape. Somehow Darcy had brought the outdoors in, and with the terrace doors open at the end of the room, had the floor not been parquetry but grass, one would've thought it was outside.

Nina dipped into a small curtsy and kissed the duke and duchess in welcome. "You've outdone yourself, Darcy. How beautiful this ballroom is."

Darcy smiled, pride alight in her eyes. "The large trees that I've used are the ones that I'm sending to Kent to be planted in your new school grounds. The transport is booked for two days from now, so I thought I'd make use of them. I hope you like my donation to your new venture."

Tears blurred Nina's vision at the generosity of her

friends. "Thank you, I'm overwhelmed by your kindness. The children will love them and I shall have a plaque made up so they'll always remember who gave them such magnificent oaks."

Darcy squeezed her hand. "My pleasure, and please, go in. I'll catch up with you shortly."

Nina joined the throng, and seeing Katherine, Lady Leighton standing alone she started in her direction. "Katherine, so lovely to see you again," she said, coming to stand beside her and taking a glass of champagne from a passing footman.

"Duchess," Katherine said, dipping into a curtsy. "I heard you were back in town and joining in more with the London Relief Society. I'm very happy we'll be seeing more of you. We need more members, particularly women that hold a position of rank, to be active in charity. More people notice our cause, I think, when women like you take part."

"I heartily agree and will do all that I can to make a difference." Nina had met the countess during her first Season, as she was related by marriage to Lizzie Doherty, who had married the man Nina had been courted by that Season, Lord Wakely. Thankfully they were now happily married and living abroad. Nina thought back on that Season for a moment, realizing she seemed to be a beacon for gentlemen who ended up marrying someone else.

The thought left her uneasy, as if there was something possibly wrong with her. She had been cold and aloof that first Season, but only because she loved Andrew Hill and didn't want to marry Lord Wakely. But then Andrew had slept with her and chosen another only hours later. Maybe there was something that others saw in her that she wasn't aware of. Something negative.

"I understand you have two daughters, Your Grace. They're twins, are they not?"

The mention of her daughters, whom she'd tucked safely into bed not an hour before, made her smile. "They're five now and very active. Already they love stories and going out in the carriage. We're going to Hatchards tomorrow. I know they may be a little young, but I think they'll enjoy the outing in any case."

"You could take them to Gunter's for ices afterwards. I know my children enjoy such treats."

For a time they discussed their children and the antics that they sometimes got up to, before Nina glanced across the ballroom floor and spotted her daughter-in-law, the Duchess of Exeter. The scowl on Bridget's forehead as she made her way over to them made a feeling of foreboding lodge in Nina's abdomen. She steeled herself for the confrontation that was without doubt soon to follow.

"Your Grace," Lady Leighton said, as Bridget reached their side. Nina raised her brow and fought to bring forth a welcoming smile for Bridget, who still had a face that was set in stone.

"A school, Nina? If it were not embarrassing enough that I have a mother-in-law who is younger than myself, now we have to live with the knowledge that you're opening a school in Kent. How could you do this to the family?"

Nina rolled her eyes. Bridget was a short woman, especially compared to the duke, who was a good foot and a half taller than her. She also was full figured and her gowns seemed too frilly, too pretty for a woman of her age. No matter how many times Nina had tried to help her gain a little fashion sense, she seemed stuck in her debutante years when her mother used to dress her up.

"There is no shame in helping those less fortunate. My opening a school will not bring embarrassment to the family. However, your public airing of your disdain for my venture may. Perhaps you ought to call the day after tomorrow and we can discuss this in private."

Bridget had the smarts to look about and see a few of the guests watching them. Her cheeks reddened. "I will not call—we have nothing to say. But if you think you're going to open a school, I want to notify you that this will not happen. Not while I'm the Duchess of Exeter."

"Well, my dear, I'm the dowager Duchess of Exeter and I do not answer to you. Now run along. This conversation has concluded." Nina lost all pretence of calm and glared at her daughter-in-law. The woman was as nasty as her husband, who had also never approved of the duke marrying her. Not that Nina cared a fig what either of them thought, but it vexed her that Bridget would snarl at her in such a public place. That she would not stomach.

"I will call tomorrow after all," Bridget said, turning away.

"You may call tomorrow but we'll not be home. I said the day after tomorrow."

Bridget didn't bother to reply, just huffed off, and Nina took a calming breath when she lost sight of her in the throng of guests.

"I'm so sorry, Your Grace. I've never seen anyone react to charity in such a negative way. Is the duchess always so toward you?" Lady Leighton asked.

Nina took a sip of her champagne, knowing she may need a few more tonight if Bridget was present. "She's always so. No matter what I do or say it is never good enough for them. As you may have heard, the duke was quite a lot of years older than me, and they never approved.

They thought I married him for his money, but it was in fact an equal arrangement, both in financial and emotional terms."

"I hope you don't find my next question prying, and please tell me if I've overstepped my mark, but I understand that you've kept the estate in Kent and the duke gifted you his second London home. Do you think the current duke found the terms of his father's will too generous, and so they intend to strike at you in any way they can?"

Nina shrugged, having had the same thought many times. But what was done was done, and the current duke knew very well that Nina had brought a fortune to the family, a portion of it allowing him and Bridget to live very comfortably. If they had any smarts between them they ought to be polite, and leave her well alone.

"Possibly, but the Kent estate was not entailed, nor was the London home. It used to be the duke's mistress's home, not that the ton knew since it's located in Mayfair. The duke and duchess may harbor some anger over losing those properties, but it's not as if they don't have many more to keep themselves occupied. The duke had multiple estates in England and Scotland."

Lady Leighton chuckled. "Then they are simply spiteful and I shall not venture to invite them to any future events at our home. And I shall talk to my friends as well and ensure they feel the coldness that can be heaped on people when they mistreat someone who does not deserve it. You opening a school is a wonderful thing, and if the current Duchess of Exeter did something similar, maybe her life would be more fulfilled than it is right now."

Nina doubted much could fulfil the duchess's life, but she nodded in agreement in any case. "I'm sure you're right."

They were soon joined by Lord Leighton, who whisked his wife out for a waltz. Nina stood alone, content to observe the guests and enjoy her champagne. Tomorrow couldn't come soon enough, and she looked forward to spending time with her girls.

"You seem lost in thought, Duchess. I hope the ball isn't boring you too much?" Mr. Byron Hill said against her ear, sending a delicious shiver down her spine. She stepped away, giving them distance and praying he hadn't noticed her reaction to him.

"Simply watching and thinking. I'm taking my children out tomorrow and I find I cannot wait. I've been so busy with the Season that they're woefully overdue for an adventure."

"That sounds like a wonderful idea," Byron stated.

He smiled, and the gesture made the small dimple on his left cheek stand out. Nina stared at it for a moment, knowing both brothers had one but on opposite sides of their faces. The night she'd slept with Andrew she could've sworn it was on the left, not the right side of his face...

"Duchess, are you well?" Byron reached out and touched her arm and Nina shook the thought aside. Now she was being silly, her memory playing tricks on her.

"I'm perfectly well, thank you. Tell me, where is your fiancée tonight? I have not seen her."

Byron rubbed a hand over his jaw, looking out toward the throng of guests. "Her father summoned her back to Cornwall so she'll miss the remainder of the Season. We're to marry in the church in her village, so I will travel there once the Season has come to an end."

Despair swamped her at the mention of Byron leaving and she took a moment to steady her emotions before she said, "And so we shall never see you again. Please do not become a stranger like you did these past years. Now that I have you back, I'm loathe to lose you again." She stared up at Byron and read the awareness that flared in his eyes. She shouldn't say such things, not to a man who loved another, but she also couldn't help herself. If only she'd seen him sooner. Had seen his worth before his course was set.

He tore his gaze from her, the muscle in his jaw flexing. "We have the Season, my friend. Let us make a promise to enjoy it together as much as we can, before I'm to Cornwall and you're back to Kent on your new adventure."

Nina held out her hand. Byron looked at it for a moment before chuckling and clasping it firmly. His hands were so very large compared to her own, and the idea of them holding her, pulling her close, giving her pleasure rocked her to her core.

He shook her hand once. "Deal, Duchess?"

"Deal," she said, letting him go. "That is one understanding I'm willing to enter into."

———

Byron walked about Hatchards holding the new poetry books that the desk clerk had notified him of their arrival while he sought out other reads. The bell on the door chimed, followed by the sound of excitable children's voices. He looked up to see the dowager duchess of Exeter and her two daughters enter, the children's nursemaid following close on their heels.

He caught hold of the shelving and stared at Nina, taking in her beauty that was amplified when around her two children. The little girls took after their mama, dark haired with just the slightest curl. They ran past him and he stared after them. They were adorable. He ought to feel annoyed, slighted, that Nina had children with a man who'd not been worthy of her affection, but he could not. Nina didn't deserve his wrath. She'd been the one he and his brother had wronged, even if Byron didn't know of his wrongdoing at the time.

He needed to tell her the truth, and soon, but it wouldn't be easy. In fact, it would be one of the hardest things he'd ever do in his life.

"Byron, I forgot how much you loved reading, even though you used to feign disinterest whenever I caught you in the library."

He bowed, taking Nina's hand and kissing it. He lingered longer than he ought and then caught himself, stepping away. "You always knew me too well."

She walked about him, running her finger along the spine of the books he was perusing. "Poetry still. Anyone would think you have a heart that longs for romance."

He swallowed and hoped the heat spreading up his neck would not settle on his face. "I do not read love poetry, and you know it." He smiled down at her and she chuckled, heading off in the direction of her girls.

"Come," she said, gesturing for him to follow. "Come meet my daughters."

Nerves settled in the pit of his stomach, but he followed, wanting to meet them but unsure if they'd like him or not. The idea flitted through his mind that the girls could've been his had he fought for her the morning she announced her engagement to the duke.

The two girls sat on the floor near a front window, laughing and giggling at a book their nurse was reading to them. They were simply the most perfect little cherubs, and the pride he saw in Nina's eyes said that she thought the world of them.

"Darlings, come meet my friend, Mr. Byron Hill. Our families were friends and we grew up together. Mr. Hill and I have been the best of friends ever since."

The two little girls looked from their mama to him, and studied him in great detail. Their eyes were the same color and shape, their hair tied up in pink ribbons, and their rose-colored frocks were identical.

"They're beautiful, Nina," he whispered, taking her hand and squeezing it a little. Then he kneeled before them and held out his hand. "How do you do, Lady Molly, Lady Lora. I'm very pleased to meet you at last. Your mama speaks of nothing else."

The two girls chuckled, the sound so like their mother's laugh, but younger. "You're not supposed to talk about us all the time, Mama. Not at balls and parties. You're supposed to talk about the weather, or the latest gowns," Lora said.

Nina nodded, looking very serious all of a sudden. "You're quite right. I shall ensure I follow those rules from this day forward."

Lora nodded, seemingly pleased with her instruction on proper etiquette. Byron fell in love with them on the spot and couldn't stop taking in their sweet little features that were so like their mama's.

"Do you like books, Mr. Hill? We're picking out some new ones today," Molly said.

"You like to read then? I'm very pleased to hear it. I love reading also." Byron stood marvelling at them.

"We do like reading, sir. We especially like it when Mama is home and reads to us. She makes the funniest sounds with some of the stories she reads to us," Lora said mischievously.

Nina chuckled and Byron didn't think he could've loved a

woman more. He remembered the exact moment he had fallen in love with her, the year before her first Season. They had been riding horses at her parents' country house and she had come off, landing hard in a puddle of mud. Most women in her situation would've screamed at the ruination of their gowns, or about the silly horse that had not behaved, but not Nina. She had laughed, laughed so hard that tears had slipped down her muddied cheeks. She'd slapped the puddle, dirtying her gown more, and Byron had laughed along with her. Had fallen in love on the spot and had never fallen out of it.

He ran a hand through his hair, reminding himself that he was engaged, that he cared for another, but even he knew that wasn't the absolute truth. He was marrying Sofia simply because she was willing and her family were looking to climb the social ladder, which he could help with. He may not be titled, but his cousin was a marquess, and he was a wealthy gentleman. Their daughter and their family would be elevated by the union.

But there was no love. No affection. In all truth, had they not been caught up with the beauty of southern France, the aquamarine water that had lapped at their boat lulling them into false ideals, they probably wouldn't have become engaged.

Being here and now with Nina, standing before what his future could be if only he tried to win her love, won out over his desire to settle. How could he allow Sofia to marry a man who loved someone else? That would not be fair to her or him, and their marriage would not be a happy one should he allow the façade to continue. He'd wronged Nina once, but he would not do it a second time, and he would not wrong Sofia either. It was time he stopped making mistakes.

"Those are the best stories of all. Now, I shall leave you to find your books." Byron bowed toward the duchess and moved off to search for more reading material, but his mind was a whirr of thoughts about what he had do to and how he would do it.

Sofia and her family would not be pleased, and he may have to offer some sort of financial settlement to get out of the contract. If Sofia wouldn't let him break the agreement he wasn't sure what he would do. Surely since there was no love, she would not be so upset. Annoyed maybe, but not enough to hold him to his promise.

He cringed.

"Byron, are you well? You seem troubled."

He didn't turn toward the duchess. They were in a secluded part of the store, hidden by bookcases. The sound of customers talking whispered to them, but still, they were alone. Quite alone...

"I'm well. You should return to your children. We'll have time to see each other at the Duncannons' ball this evening." *Please leave. Leave before I take you in my arms and kiss you like I've longed to do for five years.*

Her hand settled on his arm and he stilled. How he missed her touch. It was a form of torture and pleasure all in the one moment. Too much and yet not enough.

"We're going for ices, Byron. Join us. The girls would love for you to come." She paused for a moment before she added, "And so would I."

He turned and faced her, and his gaze shifted to her lips and wouldn't budge. He wanted to kiss her, he wanted her and no one else, had done so for too many years to count. The air in the secluded space they found themselves in thickened, and as if sensing the possibility of them being more than friends, Nina stepped away, starting back toward where her daughters were sitting.

"I will not take no for an answer, Byron." She gestured for him to follow and he could not deny her anything.

Their time at Gunter's was a trip worth taking. Over the hour he sat with Nina and the girls he learned all about their hobbies. Molly enjoyed her pony, while Lora loved dogs and especially the family wolfhound named Bentley that she spoke incessantly about, saying sweet things about how he would be terribly sad and missing them since they were at Gunter's and he was back at the townhouse. Molly had persuaded her mama to allow her to bring her pony to London with them, and before Byron departed, he agreed to take her riding, and to meet Bentley as well. Lora wouldn't have it any other way.

The duchess walked him to the pavement while the girls finished their ices. Byron hailed a hackney before turning to her. "Thank you for allowing me to meet your daughters, and for the ices. I had a wonderful time."

She looked up at him. Her hair was more natural today, loosely tied atop her head with a few wisps floating about her face, framing her perfect features. He fisted his hands at his sides before he did something stupid like reach up and clasp her jaw and kiss her.

"I'm glad you met them. It was time you did."

Byron nodded and bowed, then turned to go. She clasped his arm and he halted, loathing himself for the way his body all but jumped out of his skin each time she was near.

"I will see you tonight?" she asked, her voice cautious.

"You will," he said, and was relieved when she released his arm so he could go. Should he look at her now, turn and face her, there was little chance he would hold onto his morals, to his promise to Sofia, and not take the duchess in his arms. A place she belonged and nowhere else. He would make plans to travel to Cornwall. He needed to speak to Sofia and, if necessary, make a monetary settlement to her family for the wrong he was about to inflict on them. But he could not go on and not be true to himself. He was still in love with Nina, of that there was no doubt. Once he returned to town he would pursue her, make her see that it was him all along who was made for her. That he was the man she'd always loved, not just as a friend.

He waved to the duchess and banged on the roof to notify the driver to drive on. The awareness that was mirrored in Nina's eyes told him, more than ever before, that he may have a chance to win her. That she too had sensed the change in their comradeship, and that the friendship they'd always had had now altered into something so much more.

CHAPTER

SIX

Nina sat on a settee that had been placed on the terrace of her London townhouse and watched the girls run about the lawn, Bentley never far behind them. Their giggles and squeals of delight made her laugh, but her mind was elsewhere. Was in fact in Cornwall, where Byron had travelled the day after they met for ices at Gunter's.

He'd never said a word about it at the ball that same evening. She bit her bottom lip, not for the first time wondering what he was doing there. Of course she knew he was seeing Sofia. Would he return to town as a married man?

Andrew too had left for a country house party—odd, for it was still early in the Season—so she couldn't ask him what he knew of his brother's sudden departure.

The book she was reading by Frances Burney had not gained her attention and she placed it on the chair, sick and tired of herself and her muddled thoughts. What did it matter if Byron married sooner than he'd planned? Maybe he'd been missing his fiancée, and wanted to see her again.

Perhaps he would return to town with her accompanying him.

All the images those scenarios brought forth in her mind left little ease and she frowned, cross at herself and at him for reasons she wasn't really ready to admit to.

"Your Grace, the Duchess of Athelby to see you."

"Bring her to the terrace, thank you," she said to the footman.

Nina sighed in relief at the distraction. Anything but to be tormented a moment longer by her own musings. She stood, and smiled as the duchess stepped out onto the terrace.

"Nina, how lovely to see you," Darcy said, kissing her cheek and sitting on the vacant settee beside Nina's.

"You too. I'm so very grateful for your company. As much as I love my girls, I'm simply torturing myself with my own mind and need a friend to confide in. Your arrival is timely."

The duchess reached out and placed a hand atop hers. "Whatever is the matter, dearest? You seem quite agitated."

"That's because I am. I don't know what's wrong with me. I feel sick to my stomach. I want to get in a carriage and see something that is bothering me for myself and then decide what to do. I want to wish away coming back to town. I want..."

"You want what?" Darcy asked, her brows raised.

Nina met her gaze and read the amusement twitching her lips. "I..." She shook her head, not believing she was going to say what she was. "I want... I want Byron Hill to be mine and not Sofia Custer's. I want him with everything that I am, and I cannot have him. We've been friends for so many years, so much has happened."

"You have not... Not when he's still betrothed to Sofia, I hope."

"No, of course, not," Nina said, her cheeks heating. "But I wanted to. So many times I've wanted to throw myself at his head. You knew years ago I was fixated with his brother, but I wonder at that now. I question my motives there. Andrew had always been the polite, safe sibling if ever one was to marry into that family, and so like all the ladies, I focused my attention on him. But it was Byron that I laughed with. Who I danced with, who went riding in the park with me. We read books and sought each other out at balls and parties. I wonder now if it was Byron I always loved, and wouldn't admit to it. I chose the safe option, when I really should have gambled my heart on the brother who was wild, fierce, and passionate. The last I'm yet to explore, but I want to. I want to so much it hurts." There. She'd said all that had been plaguing her, and damn the consequences. If she were an unlikable woman then so be it.

Darcy gasped, her eyes bright with comprehension. "Well, that is something to have bottled up inside yourself. And I promise your secret is safe with me, always. But he's engaged, dearest. There is little chance that will change. What options do you have other than to love him from afar?"

Nina flopped back onto her chair, checking the girls' whereabouts and seeing they were digging in Mr. Gregory's rose bushes. The head gardener would not be pleased. "I have no options. I will not come between anyone, least of all my dearest friend's choice of bride. Even so..." She sighed. "I've been such a fool when it came to him. I see that now and unfortunately it is too late."

"Did I ever tell you that the duke and I were once best

friends too? Many years ago, before his brother passed away. But then he changed, became jaded and opinionated toward everyone, and we didn't like each other much for some time." Darcy was quiet for a minute, watching Nina's girls before she turned and met her gaze. "And yet now he is my husband, I adore the ground he walks upon and he too me. Life has a way of figuring itself out. Until Mr. Hill is married, there is always a chance."

Nina wished she could tell Darcy the whole truth—that the girls were really Andrew Hill's, not the duke's, and should Byron find out, he'd never forgive her. Even with her choices as limited as they were after Andrew proposed to another woman, Nina should have told Byron of her troubles. He would have helped her, she was sure.

"Perhaps you are right. I simply will stop worrying until I see him next. He may have visited his betrothed and nothing more."

"Do you know when he's due back?"

Nina shook her head, having not heard a word from him. "No. He's been gone some weeks now. Maybe he's decided to stay in Cornwall and not return for the Season?" The idea shot panic through her and she clasped her stomach to stop its churning. She really needed to seize hold of her emotions, or when she did see him next he'd read her like a book. He'd always had the ability to know what emotional state she was in at any moment.

"Nina, he'll return. I think the best thing you could do is to see what has happened while he was away and decide your next step from there. If he's married then there is nothing you can do, but if he is not, well, there is time. Not that I would suggest you step between them, as that would never do, but to simply see what has occurred and decide your own path. Do not forget there are many other eligible gentlemen in town who'd love to court you."

The very idea roiled through her like a poorly tasting wine. "I didn't come back to town to find a husband. That Byron returned was simply a stroke of good luck. The idea of being courted by any other men does not interest me."

Darcy sat up, clapping her hands. "You need a diversion. Something fun and a little risqué."

The idea was not uninteresting, and Nina turned her full attention toward the duchess. "What kind of diversion?"

"I have a friend, someone I've known for many years, who holds little outings for members of the *ton*. You dress up as a woman of little means—perhaps how scullery maids may dress when they go out. We take a carriage to a less refined locale in London, but a safe one I should stress, and you enjoy a night in a tavern like the common man. I've taken part in one previously, before I married the duke, and it was such fun. He will insist on accompanying me this time, but you will enjoy yourself. You drink at a bar! If you can believe that. We may gamble and dance. Let me organise this for you and our friends and we'll make a night of it."

Nina had never heard of such a thing, but it did sound like a laugh and she so needed to laugh again. To enjoy one night where she didn't have to be the grand dowager duchess, the epitome of standards. What a fake she was half the time, and the *ton* had no idea.

"I will do it. Say it will be soon. I need a diversion."

Darcy stood and held out a hand to pull Nina to stand. "I will return home now and make the arrangements. Wait for a missive from me and that will explain all."

BYRON MADE IT BACK TO LONDON LATE FOUR WEEKS AFTER HIS departure. The sojourn to Cornwall had been a welcome reprieve from town life, but the termination of his betrothal to Sofia had not been easy or well received. Which, he mused, was understandable.

He sat outside the Duchess of Exeter's London home, where most of the windows glowed with the flickering candlelight inside. Another carriage pulled up before his and the sound of laughter and animated conversations floated on the air.

The front door of Nina's home opened, and he watched as a scullery maid walked down the steps. Yet there was something about the maid that gave him pause. Her gait wasn't that of a woman who served her betters—this woman sauntered with grace, her chin held high and her posture perfect. The weathered gown went some way to disguise her, and yet he would know Nina anywhere. And right now, Nina was going out dressed as a servant.

Why the hell would she do that?

She jumped up into the carriage and Byron ordered his driver to follow them. They made their way out of Mayfair and toward Southwark before pulling up before the Talbot Inn. His own equipage pulled up across the road and Byron watched as the Duke and Duchess of Athelby exited, along with Nina. Within a minute another carriage arrived, this one bearing his own cousin and wife along with the Earl and Lady Leighton.

Byron shut his mouth with a snap, having not the slightest idea what his cousin was doing there dressed as a man of little means. Had they all lost their minds? He glanced down at himself, his highly starched cravat and perfectly pressed waistcoat. He could not enter the tavern dressed like this—he would be set upon within the first few minutes.

Ripping off his coat, he flung it on the seat across from him, before untying his cravat and loosening a couple of buttons at his neck. The waistcoat soon followed, and then he jumped out of the carriage, pulling his shirt out of his buckskin breeches. Ruffling his hair, he ordered his driver to return home, then headed toward the tavern.

No doubt he still appeared well-to-do, but it was better than a gentleman who looked ready for a ball. The tavern door tinkled as he pushed it open, and he glanced up to see a little brass bell. The room was hazy with smoke, and the stench of male sweat permeated the air.

He came up to the counter and ordered a beer before scanning the space, trying to see Nina and her friends. He heard her laugh before anything else. Moving his attention along the bar, he spotted the group standing before the bar almost at the other side of the room, each with a beer in their hands.

Byron smiled. The group of friends really did look ridiculous, but he supposed it was an escape from their lofty reality. If only everyone in such establishments could have their escape, then head back to their opulent lifestyle and houses.

Nina spotted him as he made his way over to them. Her eyes brightened with pleasure and hope spiralled through him that she liked him as much as he liked her. God, he hoped that was true. After the atrocious month he'd spent traveling to and from Cornwall, he wasn't sure he could stomach Nina turning away from what he was sure they had.

The possibility of a future.

"Byron," she said, coming over to him and wrapping her arm about his own, then pulling him toward their friends. "We're so glad to see you. Have you just returned to town?"

"I have." He nodded, taking in her beauty that was not dimmed even in the worn, tattered clothing she had on. Her face was a little flushed, whether from the warmth inside the tavern or his arrival, he wasn't sure, but he hoped it was the latter.

"You travelled to Cornwall, cousin. I hope everything is well with Sofia?" the marquess queried.

At the mention of his betrothed—now his former betrothed—Nina pulled her arm free. She picked up her glass of beer and took a sip. Did she not like the mention of Sofia? Was she jealous, perhaps? That he didn't know, but before the night was over he certainly wanted her to know the truth of his situation as it now stood. Maybe, finally, she would look at him and see *him*, and no one else.

"Sofia and her family are all in good health." Byron took a glass of beer from the Duke of Athelby, thanking him.

"When will the wedding take place, or are you here tonight to tell us you're already married?" the Duchess of Athelby asked, looking between him and Nina. Did Darcy suspect something concerning him and the duchess? His reaction toward Nina, as though his skin sizzled and his heart wanted to jump out of his chest, was certainly obvious to him—maybe it was noticeable to others too.

"I'm not married." He met Nina's eyes, wanting her alone. Where they could talk.

Unfortunately as the night wore on they didn't have any opportunity to be alone. Their antics took them to two more taverns before they eventually called it a night and hailed hackney cabs to take them home. The couples bundled themselves into individual vehicles, and finally

Byron and Nina were the only two left waiting for the next hackney to drive past.

"I'll return you home to ensure you arrive safely, Your Grace," Byron said. "If you're in agreement, of course."

She threw him a grin, her eyes sparkling from too much beer and spirits, but never had she been so beautiful to him. Somehow in her plain gown, her hair lying about her shoulders, and limited jewels, she was the Nina he knew before their very first Season. The carefree, happy girl who blossomed into a beautiful woman.

"Aya, is that a duchess? Oy, lads, we 'ave a duchess over here." Byron turned to see a group of men come from a darkened alley beside the tavern. Slowly, he reached for the small folding pen knife in his breeches pocket that he carried with him always, and held it beside his leg, not wanting to show the assailants that he was armed. Little as that arming was.

"We want no trouble, lads. This woman isn't a duchess, but only a duchess to me. My pet name for her, if ye know what I mean." Byron tried to sound like the men, and hoped by their hesitation that maybe his foolery tricked them. His hope was short-lived when one of the men at the back of the group stepped forward.

"Ay, they 'ave money. Look at her earbobs. They're a pretty set that would feed us for a year I'd say."

Byron turned to see Nina and cringed as the single diamond on each of her ears glistened beneath the street lamp. "Paste, boys. We canna afford anything else, and it was a present to my wife. Dinna take them from her."

The men glanced between him and Nina, before two drunk gentlemen stumbled out of the inn, defusing the situation. They took one more look at the earbobs and turned toward the tavern's door. "Right ye are. No hard feelings, cobba. We'll leave ye to yourself."

Relief poured through him and he reached for Nina, pulling her into his arms. Her body shook against his, and he tightened his hold, rubbing his hands along her back to try to fight away her fear.

"It's alright, Nina. They're gone now." A hackney turned up the road and Byron hailed it, bundling her inside and calling out the direction for home before anyone else could accost them. Had the men attacked, Byron wouldn't have known what to do. One against seven was too much for any man, and the men from this part of London did not play fair. More than likely someone would've been killed, possibly him or Nina.

Byron sat beside her and pulled her into the crook of his arm. He inspected her, if only to ensure she was unharmed, and she glanced up. Their gazes locked, held, and for the life of him he could not look away. He wanted her more than air right at this moment, and it would be so easy to lean in and take her lips, kiss her until they lost themselves in each other.

"You'll be home soon. There is nothing to fear now," he whispered, clasping her cheek. Unable to stop himself, he leaned down, wanting to kiss her, show her there were other things to think about, more pleasurable things, than thugs in the cesspit of Southwark.

She wrenched herself out of his arms, sliding toward the window. "You should not do that, Byron. We're friends and you're betrothed. I'll not be part of a scandalous affair even if I am a widow and can do whatever I choose."

He ran a hand through his hair. Damn it, in his fear he'd forgotten to tell her his news. "When I said earlier tonight that I'm not married, what I really wanted to say was that

I've dissolved the marriage contract. There is no longer an understanding between me and Miss Custer."

Nina stared at him with the widest eyes and he fought not to smile at her shock. He supposed such news wasn't what she or anyone would expect to hear.

"You're not marrying Miss Custer?"

"No, I'm not. The contract between our families was never a match made out of love or affection. They wished to increase their foothold within society. I had a marquess as a cousin and I needed to marry. It was time that I settled and started a family of my own. We met abroad and I am fond of Sofia, but mild friendship was only ever the depth of the emotion that passed between us."

Not expecting it, he gasped as Nina shifted back beside him, clasped his jaw and kissed him. Hard. He moaned as her mouth opened to his, her tongue sliding against his own and sending heat straight to his loins. He wrenched her onto his lap, taking her mouth in a punishing kiss. With every nip, every slide of his lips against hers, the entanglement of their tongues was punishment for not wanting him. Of choosing his straightlaced brother over him and this passion that fired between them.

Nina tasted of beer and spirits, a unique sweetness, and he couldn't get enough. Her hip settled against his sex and whether she knew it or not, her small undulations rocked him with pulse-pounding desire. He wanted to bury himself inside her. Push her, take her until they both shattered into a million pieces of pleasure.

The carriage rocked to a halt and somewhere in the recesses of his mind he heard the driver jump down off the box to open the door. He set Nina on the seat beside him. Their breathing was ragged, Nina's eyes full of unsatisfied need that he too could understand.

The door opened and without a word Nina stepped down. He watched her go inside her home, then gave the driver the new address. Hell...that kiss. That kiss was everything he'd always wanted, and it would be the first kiss of many if he could persuade her.

He'd always known there was unfulfilled desire between them, and that kiss proved it. But did it mean that Nina would give him a chance? That he wasn't certain, but he was sure as hell going to find out.

CHAPTER
SEVEN

The following week Nina stood with the Duchess of Athelby at the Keppells' ball and watched Byron from across the room. He was standing with his cousin the marquess, and both appeared quite engrossed in their conversation.

After their kiss last week in the carriage, Nina had done everything she could to avoid him. Not because she didn't want to see him, for she did, more than anything else, but because her infatuation with her best friend wasn't something she'd thought would ever happen. Not to mention that loving the two brothers made her look flippant and easy to lead.

She hated to imagine what their set would think if they heard whispers about an affair with Byron. They would probably think she had moved on to the other sibling simply because she had not gained the other's hand in marriage all those years ago. Nothing could be further from the truth. Byron, for all his wild nature, was a kind and generous friend and her affection for him had changed over time, moved on from benign camaraderie to something so much more.

Nina turned her attention away from Byron, her mind a whirr. She wanted him, but that did not necessarily mean to have him as her husband. To marry again wasn't something she wanted to do, certainly not at this moment in time. She was happy to be a mother to her girls, the master of her own domain. To become someone's chattel, no matter how much she adored Byron, wasn't a situation she strived for.

Would Byron be happy with a love affair and nothing more? He'd broken off his betrothal for her, when all was said and done. For her to turn about now and say he could share her bed but not her life seemed cruel, a waste of his love. He wanted a wife, children of his own. So much more than she was willing to give.

"What is wrong, Nina? You seem very distracted," the Duchess of Athelby said, catching her gaze.

She was distracted. More than she had ever been before. With Byron her body came to life, he made her laugh, made her smile. He made her happy, but would she make him so? "Is it so obvious?"

The duchess chuckled. "To me it is. To others, probably not. You've always been the best of friends with Mr. Hill. You've not been so obvious in your study of him to be noticeable by others, but I know how close you two were in the past, and how close you've become this Season with his return to town."

"He's no longer engaged. His trip to Cornwall saw him end his association with Miss Custer. From what I can gather they were not pleased, and given the situation I'm surprised that there isn't more talk about it in town."

"There isn't talk because he's the marquess's cousin,

and they're friends. Mr. Hill has friends that include us, dukes and duchesses and the like. I doubt there would be many who would naysay him, but there is an undercurrent of scandal, never doubt it. Some homes will never forgive him for abandoning Miss Custer."

"What are your thoughts on the matter? Are you so very angry at him? At me?"

Darcy studied Byron for a moment before she shook her head, smiling a little. "No, I'm not angry with either of you, and we shall stand by you both as your friends. You know I was married before the duke to a man I'd prefer to forget. Such marriages, ones made out of duty and even boredom, never thrive. I would not wish that for Mr. Hill and I certainly never wished it for you. You above anyone else in our friends set would know what it is like to marry a man that you do not love."

Nina knew only too well what that was like. It was a form of torture. To have them touch and kiss you when you were not physically attracted to them left you feeling dirty, assaulted even. As kind as the duke was, she did not like him in a romantic light and it caused their times in private to be very awkward and quick.

She glanced over to where Byron was and saw that he and the marquess had moved on to another set of gentlemen, one of them Darcy's husband the duke. "I think Mr. Hill ended his understanding with Miss Custer because of me," Nina said, relieved to have said aloud to a friend what had been bothering her for a week. If the *ton* found out there was something brewing between them so soon after his understanding had ended with Miss Custer, there would be rampant speculation and gossip. Her stomach twisted into knots.

"What makes you say such a thing? From what

Cameron has told me after speaking to Mr. Hill, there wasn't any affection with either party. The Custers may be put out now over the situation, but when they see Miss Custer marry a man she truly loves, I think they'll see the sense behind the decision."

"I hope so," Nina said, greeting two elderly matrons who walked past them. "But there is something else I need to speak to you about. I feel I can't disclose this to anyone else, since it's of a delicate matter."

"You can tell me anything, my dear. I'll never break your trust."

Nina pulled Darcy to a more secluded part of the ballroom and they sat in a vacant settee. She took a fortifying breath before she said, "On our way home last week from our outing in Southwark, we were accosted by a group of thugs before hailing our hackney."

Darcy gasped, and Nina clasped her hand. "Be assured all is well, and Byron was able to convince them to leave us alone. But I was very upset. I thought we were in trouble that was beyond our scope to get out of. In the carriage on the way home, I don't know whether it was because I was upset, or whether it was because Byron wanted to comfort me, help me over the ordeal, but..." She paused for a moment as her body reacted to the memory of his kiss. Of how everything bad that had happened to her up to that moment disappeared and it was like the sun came out and all would be right in the world. "We kissed. Actually, it wasn't a kiss. It was so much more than a kiss." She closed her eyes, wanting to do it again, if only to see if the emotions he brought forth in her were real. Never had she ever had such a reaction to a man, not even Andrew, and she'd thought herself in love with him.

Byron was her oldest, dearest friend. To feel passion in his arms wasn't what she expected at all.

Darcy grinned. "How very interesting. You enjoyed Mr. Hill's kiss then, my dear?"

Nina clasped her abdomen as butterflies fluttered in her stomach at the memory of it. "I did. So much. His kisses are as wicked as his past escapades were and I find myself now wanting to be alone with him again. When he told me that his understanding with Miss Custer was at an end, I didn't feel what one ought to feel for a friend—sadness, wanting to comfort those that are hurting. I wanted to fling myself into his arms and tell him to have me. To take me instead. And, well, I'm pretty certain that's exactly what I did."

Darcy chuckled and as a footman walked past, the duchess procured them a glass of punch each. "What do you think Mr. Hill thinks of the kiss? Do you believe him to be in agreement with your emotions over the embrace?"

Nina nodded. "I believe so, but I've been avoiding him. You know how much I wanted to marry his brother Andrew all those years ago. If I turn my attentions onto his sibling, I appear like a fool. Someone who cannot move on from their first infatuation. Not to mention I never thought to marry again, and Byron wants a wife, a family. I'm not certain I want to give up my freedom just yet."

"You are not under any time restraint, Nina," Darcy said, matter of fact. "People change in time. What you once liked you can hate in the years to come and vice versa. In time you may find that marrying Byron is exactly what you want, or you may both agree that your time together must end. Nothing is set in stone. Let your emotions guide you and I'm sure you'll do what is right."

Could they go from being friends to lovers? There was no doubt in Nina's mind that was what she wanted. She wanted Byron with a need that surpassed any she'd ever felt before. What she felt the night he'd kissed her scared her and tempted her at the same time. She could not walk away now, not when they were both free to do as they pleased, without seeing if there was a possibility for them.

"Do you think it scandalous of me to want him, more than a friend would want another friend? I want," she said, lowering her voice to a whisper, "for him to share my bed. I'm wicked I know to say such things, but I need to tell someone, or I'll simply burst and shout it out loud across the room."

Darcy laughed, sipping her punch. "While I agree with your choice, I would advise that vocalizing that across the room would be a bad idea." She smiled. "Talk to him. Tell him what you want and see what he wants in return. You're both adults. You're a widow. It's not against the rules for you to break them a little. If you're discreet."

Excitement thrummed through Nina's veins at the thought of having Byron in her bed. She looked up and caught the very man who occupied her thoughts watching her. Heat coursed through her veins and she could not look away.

Tonight he wore a superfine coat that fit his muscular figure to perfection. His cravat was perfectly tied and show-cased his tempting chiselled jaw. His dark, heated gaze seared her with intent and she licked her lips, parched all of a sudden.

Her attention slid over his form, his broad shoulders that tapered down to a narrower waist. He was a muscular man—she imagined horse riding helped keep him toned—and she couldn't help but think of what he would look like naked. It was odd to think of Byron in such a way, but now after their kiss, she did little else.

"I will talk to him. We cannot go on as we are now."

"No," Darcy said, her tone laced somewhat with sarcasm. "I fear if you did continue on in the same way as you are now, the attraction you two have for each other will be known all around London. Why, even now, Mr. Hill watches you with the intensity of a man very much smitten. Some may even say wantonly."

Nina knew all about lust—or she'd certainly learned it after kissing Byron. Not even with Andrew had she ever wanted him as much as she wanted Byron. How strange that her body knew her true feelings before her mind did. Byron had always been the gentleman she wanted, she just never realized it before now.

"I will behave and be less obvious in my admiration of the gentleman. And I think," she said, standing, "I shall seek him out now and have our little tête-à-tête. Thank you for listening, Darcy. I appreciate it."

Darcy waved her thanks away. "The pleasure was all mine. I wish you well."

Nina bit her lip, smiling. "I wish myself well too."

BYRON HAD WATCHED THE DUCHESS OF ATHELBY AND NINA talking privately, and he would've given anything to hear what their conversation involved. The hairs on the back of his neck prickled and he couldn't help but believe that they were talking about him.

His discussions on the other hand involved politics, horses, and the latest scandal rocking the *ton*. He'd debated excusing himself and going to Nina and asking her to take a stroll about the room, but instead he headed outdoors, wanting a little fresh air.

The cool night air was refreshing after being inside among a kaleidoscope of scents, and he headed to the end of the terrace and stepped down onto the gravelled path leading across the lawn.

The Keppells' home backed onto Hyde Park, and he strolled toward the little gates he knew the yard held. He would take a few minutes to regain his composure. The longer he watched Nina, the more his body reacted to her presence.

She consumed him, and yet over the past week she'd done everything in her power to avoid him. Did she regret their kiss? Was she sorry for allowing him his advances? Damn, he hoped not.

He ran a hand over his jaw as the iron gates came into view. They were locked. He stopped when he reached them, staring at the park beyond, its dark space as bleak as his own future if he did not convince Nina to be part of it.

"Byron," someone called out. He turned, his heart thumping loud in his chest at the sight of Nina walking purposefully toward him.

"Whatever are you doing out here? I saw you leave and in these slippers I wasn't as fast as you on the gravel."

He chuckled, coming to stand before her. "I needed to clear my head. A lot of scents inside." Although that was only half the reason. His true reason was standing before him, looking up at him with the biggest, bluest eyes he'd ever known. How he adored her. Her kind heart, her friendship, that she was a wonderful mother to her children.

"Yes," she said, walking past him a little to stare out at the park. "I'm sorry I've been avoiding you. I've not wanted to, but I needed to clear my head over...well, you know. What happened in the carriage."

He came and stood behind her, so close he could smell

the jasmine in her hair, and yet he did not touch her. He fastened his hands at his side to stop himself. "When we kissed," he whispered against her ear.

She shivered and wrapped her arms about her waist before she turned to face him. "Yes. When we kissed and the friendship we've had with one another changed forever."

"Has it changed forever?"

He swallowed the panic, hoping she was not about to cut him free, tell him that their embrace was a mistake. It was not an error of judgement for either of them. They were made for one another. In time he would gain her love and then he could tell her the truth of their night together all those years ago. Now wasn't the time, but he would be honest with her when she was ready to hear such honesties. Truths that would not be easy to endure.

He was being selfish in his secrecy over the night his brother had tricked them both, but he needed time to win her love. After the years that had separated them, only now were they gaining their friendship back, becoming closer with every moment they spent together. He wanted her to know his heart was true, loyal to her, when he revealed the truth. To have her repudiate him was not an outcome he could bear.

Neither of them were to blame for what had happened—that deceit lay entirely on his brother's soul —but even so, the truth would hurt Nina, and he was loathe to do that to her. His fear that she would cast him aside, that it may cause him to lose her forever, wasn't to be borne. He would tell her the truth, and soon— just not yet.

"Of course it has changed, Byron." She stepped closer still, her arms unfolding to wrap about his waist. His body sagged in pleasure and he shut his eyes for a moment, reveling in the feel of her so close to him again.

He wrapped his arms about her back. "Tell me how."

She grinned up at him. "After our kiss the other night, I've done little else but think of you, and if you're willing, I'd like for us to be lovers."

The breath in his lungs seized and he took a moment to gain his equilibrium. She wanted to be his lover. Hell yes, there was little else he wanted in return. To be with her privately, to spend time alone, was what he longed for most. Not just to have her in his bed, but to also enjoy her company. To talk, laugh, and play just as they did prior to her first Season.

He missed such days, and he'd missed her. She was giving him this chance, and he was not about to bugger it all up. He would love her, adore her, just as she should always have been loved and adored, so much so that she would never want him to leave.

"I would be honored. You have no idea how much I've wanted to be with you like that."

"You have?" she asked, grinning up at him.

Under the moonlight he could make out the slightest blush. Was she a little embarrassed to have asked him to take her to his bed? Possibly, but what a strong, independent woman she was to have done so. It only made him adore her more.

"You must know that the whole reason I asked to be released from my understanding was solely due to seeing you again. I couldn't marry Sofia when I wanted another woman altogether." Not just in his bed, but in his life. And now that Nina had given him this opportunity there was little chance he would let her go without a fight.

She reached up and wrapped her hands about the nape

of his neck, playing with a little strand of his hair. "You've been my best friend for so many years. How do we even start such an affair?"

"Like this, my darling," he said, leaning down and kissing her softly on the cheek. He kissed his way to her ear, paying attention to just below her lobe after she shivered a little in his arms at his touch. She was so soft, pliant in his arms, and had she not been tightly enfolded in his embrace, he could not have believed his turn of fortune. "And this," he said finally, kissing her lips.

She leaned up against him, her breasts hard against his chest, and she let out a little mewling sound that went straight to his groin. She opened for him like a flower in the sun and he kissed her deeply, savouring every moment, wanting more with each second that passed.

To kiss a woman with passion, a woman whom one had respected and cared for, for so many years, made the embrace different somehow. More meaningful, intimidating even. To lose this, to have her walk away when their love affair was over, simply wasn't an option. Not for him in any case.

She met his kiss with as much fire and need as his own and something squeezed in his chest. He understood the danger of kissing a woman one had an emotional relationship with. It could lead to more than simple affection—it could lead to love.

The idea didn't scare him as much as it once might have. Not with Nina at least. With this woman in his arms, he couldn't imagine anyone else who could take her place. Nor did he wish to. And if that meant that he was falling in love with her, then so be it.

He was a man in love, well and good.

CHAPTER
EIGHT

Nina lay upon her bed the following morning and stared at the ceiling. Her maid had been in earlier and drawn open the curtains, and the dappled sunlight streaming through the windows gave the room a warm, summery glow.

She grinned, her stomach turning in knots over what had happened at the Keppells' ball the evening before. The kiss she'd shared with Byron had been better than their first, and they had made plans for him to come to the Duke and Duchess of Athelby's intimate dinner this evening.

She sighed and rolled over, staring out the bank of windows that ran the full length of her room. When had she become so infatuated with him? When had he become the sole reason to attend parties and events? If she were honest with herself, the week she'd not seen him after their first kiss had been torture. She'd wanted to see him every second of every day. To take in his athletic figure, admire his sweet nature and devilishly naughty antics. He was an alluring man.

I wonder what he'll be like in bed...

The naughty thought made her grin. Tonight after dinner she may find out, if she were game enough to allow him to stay.

There was a light knock on her door and her maid bustled into the room. She bobbed a quick curtsy. "Good morning, Your Grace. The Duchess of Exeter is in the downstairs drawing room and she's saying she's not leaving until she has seen you. She seems quite agitated, Your Grace."

Nina sighed, cursing her vexing daughter in law to Hades. It was just like Bridget to arrive and ruin her good morning thoughts about a certain Byron Hill.

She dressed quickly in a light blue morning gown and joined the duchess downstairs. "Good morning, Bridget. To what do I owe the pleasure of your company so early today?" Her tone was polite, but edged with sarcasm. She checked the time, and seeing the early hour, fought to deny herself the right to tell the duchess to leave and come back again at a decent hour.

Bridget sat on the settee before the unlit hearth and glared at her. "There is talk of you about town. Talk that will impact my family and children. I'll not have it, Edwina. You need to leave for Kent, and soon."

Nina raised her brow and rang the bell, then ordered tea from the footman who entered. Only when he left the room did she reply to Bridget. "I beg your pardon, Duchess, but what makes you think I have to do anything that you tell me?" She sat on a nearby chair and folded her hands in her lap, lest they be used to strangle her daughter-in-law before her.

"We know about your less-than-proper marriage to the duke, and now there is talk you have a lover. It's embarrassing that you would stoop so pathetically low as to chase the brother of the man who denied you all those years ago."

"Who told you this falsehood?" Nina asked. How did Bridget even find out about her association with Byron? She had been very discreet and only spoken to Darcy about it, and the duchess would never break her trust.

"I need no one to tell me what I saw with my own eyes last evening. You, chasing after a man like a Covent Garden whore."

Had Bridget seen them kiss in the garden? Nina ignored her cutting remark and took a calming breath, feigning innocence. "You mean Mr. Byron Hill, I presume." Just the mention of Byron's name made her heart leap in her chest. "That I'm making a spectacle of myself by seeking him out. Have you forgotten that we have been friends since well before our first Seasons in town? That I practically grew up with him? Of course I gravitate toward him. He's the best person I know."

The duchess's cold eyes narrowed into annoyed slits. "He devours you with every glance. It is obvious to every one of our set that you're infatuated with each other, probably already lovers. Which considering your past does not surprise me or the duke."

If the duchess's words were meant to make Nina rethink her relationship with Byron, it had the opposite effect. If anything, the idea that Byron devoured her each time he looked at her filled her with unsated need.

The tea arrived and thankfully it gave Nina a moment to compose herself. How dare Bridget chastise her in such a way. She was a widow, a financially independent one at that. She may do as she pleased, and damn anyone who had a problem with her choices.

"He may wish to court me, and should I take him to my bed, I can assure you that I will be discreet."

Bridget gasped, her show of shock and outrage more

emotion than Nina had ever seen her exhibit before in her life.

"How could you! How could you sleep with a man not your husband?" The duchess levelled a finger in her direction, stabbing it into the air. "You're a harlot. You should not be in Mayfair, but in Convent Garden where all the other prostitutes hire out their services."

Anger snapped through Nina. "Do not criticize me for being a woman of independent thought and needs. And never accuse me of being a whore, when your husband no doubt takes pleasure in the arms of such women on his nights in the slums." Nina felt a pang of guilt when Bridget's face paled at her words, but then the memory of her toxic daughter-in-law's accusations pushed that aside.

Bridget's face contorted into something ugly and mean. "We know the girls aren't the duke's. How my father-in-law fell for such a ruse I'll never understand. Years ago you were rumored to be days away from announcing your engagement to Mr. Andrew Hill, but then overnight you were engaged to my father-in-law and Mr. Hill was betrothed to Miss O'Connor. You understand hasty marriages always make one question the validity behind them. Yours is no different," she said with saccharine spite.

Nina scoffed but her blood ran cold at the mention of her daughters and the fact that Bridget and the duke thought they were not George's. Did others suspect? And now with her renewed friendship with Byron, it may give such rumors even more fuel. But then, what of it? No one could prove the girls were not George's and there was nothing wrong with being friends with Byron. Even if their attachment had grown to feelings far beyond friendship. She would not cower to the woman before her—a nasty, vindictive, unhappy woman. Nina would not allow the duchess to ruin her life. Not now that she'd finally got it back and was the master of her own domain.

"Get out and do not come back here again. Neither you nor the duke are welcome in this home, which I might remind you is mine by law. You have no claim on me, or my estates. You have no right to speak my daughters' names. Do not take me for a fool or a woman who will stand for such insults. I have friends too, Bridget. Friends who would cut you out of society without hesitation should I mention this conversation."

Bridget stood, all pretence of civility gone. "I have friends too, do not forget. As for these rumors, I do not want them out in Society any more than you do. I have children who will suffer from this scandal should it get out. I suggest you end it with Mr. Byron Hill before you're caught and there isn't anything anyone can do to help you."

"I neither need nor seek your help. Leave. Now."

Bridget strode out the door and Nina picked up her cup of tea, taking a sip. What a toxic witch. She thought about Bridget's words regarding her and Byron and wondered if they were too obvious in public. Did he really look at her like he wanted to devour her whole?

A grin tweaked her lips. Yes, yes he did, and she adored that it was so. But she would adjust how she reacted to him in public if only to keep her girls away from potential scandal. She would never wish to sully them because she could not control herself when around Byron.

BYRON COOLED HIS HEELS IN THE DUKE AND DUCHESS OF Althelby's drawing room while they waited for dinner to be announced. His cousin had garnered him the invite to this private dinner hosted by the duke and duchess, and he was beyond grateful. The night was young, Nina would arrive soon, and there were limited people about, meaning he could monopolize her time and be with her. Possibly take her home and snatch a kiss or two.

The blood in his veins warmed at the thought as he listened to the marquess and duke talk about a horse going up for auction at Tattersalls that they both wanted, while keeping his attention on the drawing room door.

He didn't have to wait long. The breath in his lungs seized at the sight of Nina. Tonight she wore a gown that was pure perfection, hanging from her light frame without a flaw. The green muslin dress hugged her breasts while hinting at her shapely waist and hips. The sheer material was light in color but the undergarment was a deeper shade, making the gown shimmer with each step she took.

Byron caught her gaze and smiled. A light blush stole across her cheeks and he fought not to go to her so soon. To not be too obvious in his interest.

"She's a very beautiful woman," his cousin said, leaning toward him to ensure privacy from the other guests besides the duke.

The duke chuckled, lifting his glass in salute. "She's related to me. Good looks are a trait that we're all blessed with."

The marquess scoffed. "Darcy is beautiful. You, on the other hand, I'm certain she took pity on and nothing more."

Byron chuckled as the duke tried to argue the point but then had to concede that Darcy was indeed beautiful and he was lucky to have her as his wife.

"So," the duke said after a moment, "will Nina be the next Mrs. Hill, good man?"

Byron hoped that would be so. He'd like nothing more

than to have her as his wife. The affection he felt for her had long ago changed from friendship to so much more. His feelings were so much stronger than what he felt for her five years ago. He'd loved her then, but he adored and loved her so much more now. Seeing her as a woman, a kind, intelligent lady, who no matter her status, cared for and loved her children, put them before anyone else, made what he felt for Nina beyond anything he'd felt in his youth.

"If she'll have me, of course I'd marry her. But whatever this is between us is also very new. I do not want to rush her." He needed Nina to love him before he offered for her hand. Not because he needed the emotion to be said between them, but because without love there was no chance that she would forgive what he'd done all those years ago. Or at least, what his brother had ensured he'd done without their knowledge.

Without love he would have no chance of gaining her forgiveness. His brother last night had accosted him in the library, demanding he tell the duchess the truth of their situation. Byron would do so, and soon.

"I think she'll have you, if her admiration of you when she thinks no one is looking is any indication." The marquess grinned at him, taking a sip of his whisky. "Have you spoken at all about the possibility of a future?"

Byron nodded, finishing his drink. "We have, and we're willing to try and see. I know she's very independent and focused, especially on the new school, but I would like to help her with the school. I'd do anything to spend time with her."

The marquess slapped him on the shoulder. "Good man, you're in love with her."

The word *love* echoed in his ear and yet it did not scare him. Why not admit to one's feelings when they were true?

He did love her, had loved her for years—she simply wasn't aware of the fact. But she would be soon. Now that they were going to be lovers, he would show her every moment of every day when they were together how much he adored and valued her.

"Yes, I am," he admitted, smiling a little. "Now if you'll excuse me, I'm going to go dare a duchess to do the same."

He left the duke and marquess chuckling behind him as he went in search of Nina. He found her sipping a glass of champagne alone beside the fire, lost in thought.

He lifted her gloved hand and kissed it gently, lingering over it a moment to savor the feel of her again. "Good evening, Your Grace. You're very beautiful this evening, but I should imagine you already knew that."

Nina grinned at him, taking back her hand. "Why thank you, Mr. Hill. How very kind of you to notice."

"I notice everything about you," he whispered, coming to stand beside her so that they could talk a little more privately.

"I've missed you." His arm at his side, he reached out using the cover of his jacket and her gown to clasp her hand. Their fingers entwined and it was the most erotic move he'd ever made in his life. Of course he'd slept with women before, but to touch her in such a clandestine way, to hold Nina and no one else, even if it were only her hand, sent shocks to his heart.

He loved her possibly more than she'd ever love him. The thought gave him pause. He could be hurt by adoring her so. She was yet to learn the truth of their one night together. He hated that she would be wounded to know that his brother had tricked them both into being in the same location, under false comprehensions where neither one of them could take back what had happened. But to not take the risk of loving this woman, to have her as his, to marry and wake up next to her for the remainder of their days, was worth any risk to his heart.

She didn't pull away from his touch, and the look she bestowed on him radiated need and longing.

"I've missed you too. I also wish to speak to you about something, but not here. Will you escort me home later this evening? We need to be alone for that conversation."

"Of course," he said without a thought. A small frown line sat between her eyes and he wondered what she was thinking about. Was something worrying her? "Tell me, please, that what you wish to talk to me about later today does not involve you telling me that we cannot be together. I could not bear such an outcome. Not after the other evening."

She shook her head, a few wisps of hair about her face bouncing with the movement. "It's not that. I promise."

"You seem a little down, Nina. Are you certain you want to wait until later to talk about what's bothering you? I'm sure we can find somewhere private after dinner."

The butler entered the room and, bowing to the guests, declared dinner served. The select group of guests made their way to the dining room on the opposite side of the house, and Byron found himself seated beside the Duchess of Athelby. He would've preferred to be seated beside Nina, but Darcy was lovely company and always good at keeping the conversation interesting if not amusing.

The first course came and went with general conversation and on-dits about the *ton* and what people were planning to attend during the coming weeks. Byron listened and kept watch on Nina, who was seated on the opposite side of the table and further along. Her conversation with his cousin the marquess seemed pleasant, but there was little doubt that something was on Nina's mind and it was troubling her.

"Is everything well with Nina, Mr. Hill? She seemed a little distant before we came in to dine," the duchess said as she continued her meal.

Byron sighed, having himself been pondering that question. "I'm to escort her home this evening, and she mentioned that there is something that she wished to speak to me about, but wouldn't tell me what that was. I hope she is well. I do not like to see her so distracted."

"I should think not." The duchess threw him an amused glance. "Come, Mr. Hill. It is obvious to all of us here, your friends I might add, that you're smitten with Nina. And why would you not be? You've known her for many years, were the best of friends prior to her marriage to the duke. When you have a connection with someone that is linked and fused in friendship, it is sometimes a natural progression into love."

Having taken a sip of his drink, Byron coughed, almost choking on his wine at the duchess's bold words. "You have a lovely table decoration, Your Grace," he said, hoping that his change of subject would be hint enough that he didn't want to discuss him and Nina any further. What was between him and Nina was private and very, very new. He didn't want their friends to become too involved when he himself was still navigating their blossoming relationship.

"Very well, I will drop the subject. But as for Nina's difficulties, I think you'll find that she is having problems with her daughter-in-law, the Duchess of Exeter. I heard a rumor today that the duchess is quite put out about Nina opening a school in Kent, and I also heard your name mentioned."

"What?" he said, adjusting his tone when the Duke of

Athelby looked down the table and met his gaze. "I beg your pardon, Your Grace, but why would anyone be talking about me? I'm no one of importance."

"You are a dowager duchess's best friend, you're male, and she's a widow. There is talk."

Byron cringed. Of course, the meddling Duchess of Exeter was causing trouble for Nina because of her association with him. Well, he wouldn't have it. How dare anyone try and tell them that they could not see each other, or be friends. Now that he was at liberty to do so, he would court Nina, or anyone else for that matter, if he wished to, and no vicious gossiping witch would tell him that he could not.

"Thank you for letting me know. I'll be sure to adjust my behaviour when next we're seen together in the *ton*."

"You would stop courting Nina? You cannot," Darcy said, throwing him a glance as arctic as her husband's just before.

Byron chuckled, slicing into his beef with more force than was necessary. "Oh no, I'm not adjusting my actions to be less noticeable, but to be more so. I'm nothing if not stubborn when told that I cannot have what I want. And between you and me, Duchess, I want Edwina and I will prove to her that she wants me as well. Not just as a friend, but as a husband."

Darcy patted his arm, smiling. "I knew I was not wrong about you. I have faith that you will succeed."

Byron looked down the table and caught Nina's eye, smiling. He would succeed. Failure in this situation was not an option. "I have faith that I will as well."

CHAPTER
NINE

On the way home from the Duke and Duchess of Athelby's dinner party, Nina sat beside Byron as they made their way through the Mayfair streets toward her townhouse. Her driver would take Byron home after she was delivered safely to her door. She frowned, staring out at the streets beyond, wondering how to tell Byron about her dreadful daughter-in-law's accusations today.

How humiliating that she would have to tell him such things. How awful that the *ton* was gossiping about them like they were having a clandestine affair, which they were not. Not yet at least. If she were going to be accused of something she at least wanted to be guilty of it.

"I wanted to talk to you in private because today I had a visit from—"

"I know who visited you today, and you do not need to explain anything. We're going to ignore the duchess and her viperish tongue and do as we please." He took her hand, unbuttoning her glove from her elbow down before sliding it off. A shiver stole through her body at having him so close to her again. Just the two of them with no one else about to distract them or stop what was inevitable.

"I don't care if we're fodder for town gossip. All I care about is you."

His words were like a repairing elixir, one she'd needed from the moment Bridget had stormed out of her parlor this morning. "Because I threw myself at your brother all those years ago, now it looks as if I'm throwing myself at you. She labeled me a harlot. Someone who cannot let go of the past."

Byron shifted closer to her, wrapping his arm about her shoulder and pulling her in close to his side. "We were the best of friends long before you fell for my brother, which I do believe was nothing but a passing youthful fancy that you grew out of. What we have together, what I feel for you, do not let some nasty, unhappy duchess ruin. I will not leave you alone, I will not leave again, if that is your fear."

Tears prickled in her eyes, and she blinked to clear her silliness away. Byron reached up and wiped a stray tear from her cheek, and she sniffed. "I'm sorry. I don't know why I'm being so emotional over what Bridget said. I shouldn't let her get to me in such a way, but she made me feel cheap. Made me believe the *ton* would look down on my girls for my allowing a gentleman to court me."

"No," he said, shaking his head. "You are a beautiful woman, too young to be a matron, and too sweet to be seen as anything other than wonderful. Your children would want you to take a chance, to possibly find love. I want you to take that chance with me." Byron studied her a moment and she wondered what he was debating saying. "I—"

"What?" she asked when he didn't say anything further. "Tell me what you were going to say."

He clasped her chin, lifting her face up as if he were

about to kiss her, but instead he said, "I've always adored you. When I saw you with my brother all those years ago it used to drive me to distraction. I would act out, create scandals, gamble and drink, flirt with young and old. And it was all because I wanted you and you were looking the other way. I thought that if I created enough noise you would see me. It should have been me you married. Not Andrew and not the Duke of Exeter, but *me*."

The breath in Nina's lungs seized and a little piece of her died at knowing that he'd longed for her, but in her youthful idiocy she'd not seen him as anything other than her friend. How could she have been so blind?

"I see you now," she said, clasping the lapels of his jacket. She fisted her hands about the fabric and pulled him close. "And I'm not looking in any other direction than you."

Byron growled and took her mouth in a searing kiss, one that she matched in every way. The carriage rumbled along the gravel road toward her townhouse, the London *ton* and its many entertainments passed them by beyond the carriage windows, and still the kiss continued...

With each stroke of his tongue, each nip of his teeth, the lure of them solidified within Nina and she never wanted to let go. Oh, she saw Byron now, he was all that she did see and it was an image she'd be loathe to part from. A man of honor, a man capable of loyalty, friendship, and love. A kind, passionate soul who was a match for her in every way.

The thought that should he know who the father of her girls really was lingered in the back of her mind, but she pushed it away. Surely he would forgive her for the falsehood, understand that she'd had little option but to marry the duke when Andrew had abandoned her after their night together.

She kissed Byron with all the passion she could muster, and after weeks of being near him again, of watching him, longing for him, the ferocity with which they touched was enough to singe her skin.

"Touch me," she begged when his hands stubbornly refused to move from her cheeks.

She clasped his hand and placed it upon her breast, moaning at the pure delight that his touch evoked. She'd wanted him to touch her there, ached in the dead of night for him to fill and inflame her.

His hand cupped her breast through her gown, and sliding his hand over her puckered nipple, he rolled it between his thumb and forefinger. "You're so beautiful, my darling. I never wish for this night to end."

Nina threw her head back as his other hand slid down her back, pulling her closer still. He kissed his way down her neck, the touch of his tongue gliding over the lobe of her ear making her gasp.

"You tease," she said, laughing a little. "I don't want you to tease me. I want you to take me to your bed."

He nipped her shoulder, kissing down the front of her chest, before he sat back a little, his hand going to the top of her gown and slipping it down to reveal her breast. The cool night air kissed her skin, and for moment she watched Byron as he gazed at her, the need and hunger in his brown orbs making the ache between her thighs double.

"So exquisite." He leaned down and kissed her nipple, a soft, closed-mouth kiss before his tongue darted out and he licked it once. "Do you like that, my love?"

She nodded, unable to form words as she watched him pay homage to her breast. He kissed her nipple again, this time opening his mouth. The heat of his touch seized her and without thought she clasped his head, holding him against her as he kissed and suckled her breast.

"Byron," she said during a moment of clarity. "It's not enough. I want you."

The carriage rocked to a halt, and for a moment Nina couldn't gauge where she was. Byron fixed her gown before leaning over and opening the door, then stepping down to help her alight.

"And you shall have me, Duchess, but not tonight. There are too many eyes about for me to come to you now. But I will come to you soon and we shall be discreet. I will not put you at risk of scandal. No matter how much I want you right now."

Nina didn't move from the carriage seat, partly because she didn't want to leave, and party because she wasn't sure her legs would carry her. He threw her an amused smile and held out his hand to assist her.

Reluctantly, she clasped it, thankful for the help. Coming to stand before him on the footpath, she looked up and met his eyes. The unconcealed hunger that she read in them left her nerves trembling through her body. His dark locks, a little mussed from their activity in the carriage, made her want to reach up and pull him down for another kiss. To discombobulate him as much as he had thrown her.

She touched her lips, having never had such passion before in her life, and while she understood that whatever was between them was at its beginning, she worried for when it would end. She didn't wish it to end. Something told her that having Byron Hill in her bed would be an adventure she'd crave to repeat. Would be enough to tempt her to forget her ideals of living alone for the rest of her life, content to be a mother only, and throw caution to the wind and place herself into the hands of a man. A husband.

"Goodnight, Mr. Hill," she said, stepping toward the front steps of her home.

Byron reached out and took her gloveless hand, kissing her fingers gently. "Goodnight, Your Grace."

Nina sighed, watching as he strode the couple of steps back to the carriage and jumped in. The door to her home opened, but she didn't move, simply watched as Byron's carriage pulled away into the London traffic. The sound of Molly's sweet voice sounded behind her and she turned to see her daughter standing on the staircase inside.

"Molly," she said, coming inside and handing a waiting footman her coat. "Whatever are you doing up? You should've been in bed hours ago." She reached down and picked her daughter up, and carried her upstairs.

"I had a bad dream, Mama." Molly paused, taking her in. "You look pretty, Mama. I like your dress."

Nina smiled, kissing her sweet cheek. "Thank you darling, but tell me what happened in your dream," she said, cuddling her close.

"A monster. Behind the curtain. He wanted to eat me and Lora."

"Aww, my poor little poppet. Just remember, my sweeting, that dreams are only figments of our imagination, and although they can be scary, they're not real. And Mama's home now. I'll not let anything happen to you."

Her daughter looked up at her, rubbing her eye—a sure sign she was beyond tired. "Will you sleep in our room tonight, Mama?"

Nina made for their bedroom, which was on the same floor as hers as she refused to have them too far away from her. Entering the room, she smiled as Lora sat up in her bed, seemingly wide awake as well.

"How about instead of me sleeping in here, you girls

come and sleep in my bed? It's much bigger and we can have a little catch up if you like. Would you like that?"

The girls squealed with delight, and Molly wiggled to be put down. Both girls grabbed the small dolls they had on their beds and followed Nina to her room. Nina had her fire stoked and the children settled into her bed before she joined them. Nina ordered breakfast for all three of them in her room the following morning before dismissing her maid. Then she jumped into bed between the girls and wrapped her arms about them both.

"Mama, do you want to know what my dream was about?"

"Of course," she said, and listened to Molly describe the monster who'd hidden behind the curtains. Nina took in her children's features as they chatted about the dream and how they would kill the beast that scared Molly. They were so like Andrew in looks, it was no wonder that Bridget had concluded they were not the duke's. How Byron had not caught the resemblance baffled her, but perhaps he'd not seen the girls enough. She would have to tell him the truth before he guessed himself.

With their dark locks and lithe figures, that alone put them apart from the duke. He'd been a short, round gentleman of very little height. The girls were thin and tall for their age. Not to mention there was something about their eyes that echoed Andrew's family. Even Byron had the same almond-shaped eyes as his brother, and the girls did too.

She would have to tell him, before they went any further in their relationship together. He deserved to know the truth before they started a love affair on a foundation of lies and deceit. Byron deserved better than that.

CHAPTER
TEN

B yron called on the duchess late in the afternoon two days later, bringing a posy of yellow roses, which he knew had always been her favorite flower. He was ushered into the front parlor and found her seated before the unlit hearth, reading a book.

"Byron," she said, standing and coming over to greet him.

He kissed her cheek before they sat back down on the settee.

"Tea, please, and please close the door on your way out," Nina said to the footman. He bowed and did as she bade before she turned her attention back to Byron.

Today she wore a morning gown of bright canary yellow, a color that suited her. She looked like summer and spring rolled into one and he wanted nothing more than to kiss her as if they were already married.

"You look beautiful today, Nina. You should wear yellow more often." Her cheeks flushed and she leaned back into the settee, studying him.

"I've not seen you in two days. I had started to wonder

if I had frightened you away." She chuckled, then leaned forward and kissed him. Her lips were soft and warm, and his need of her increased.

Since their parting the other evening he'd thought of little else other than having her in his bed. He longed to be the one and only man she desired, wanted, and loved, and he would do everything in his power to have her love him. For there was little doubt in his mind that he was well and truly, deeply in love with his best friend.

"You would never do so. I've thought of you constantly too."

She nodded, but something in her eyes gave him pause.

"Is there something wrong, Nina? Please tell me. I never want to see you unhappy." He took her hand, reveling in the fact she had no gloves on and he could feel her, her warmth and delicate fingers.

"I haven't been honest with you, and I fear that what I'm about to tell you will hurt you very much. So much so that whatever this is between us now will end."

The pit of Byron's gut churned with fear that he knew what she was about to tell him. Or at least what she thought to be the horrible lie that sat between them.

"Go on," he managed to say, bracing himself to listen to her side of the story.

She adjusted her seat, folding her hands in her lap. "You know that I threw myself at your brother, but what you don't know is that I offered my body to him the night before he asked Miss O'Connor to be his wife. An offer he accepted."

She stared into the fire, and he wished he could rip away the pain that he could read in her dark orbs. A pain that he had inflicted on her, if not on purpose.

"I lost my innocence that night, and the following

morning I woke to the news that he'd offered to Fionna and they were to be married in Ireland, where her family were from. I debated going to Mama and Papa and telling them what I'd done. I knew they would force his hand. And with the Duke of Athelby my cousin, I could've used his social standing to make Andrew marry me. But I realized I couldn't marry a man who'd sleep with an unmarried maid, and then turn about only hours later and offer to someone else. Such a man was not worthy of my hand."

Byron clenched his jaw closed, his mind and heart arguing over what he ought to do and what he would do. Should he tell her the truth, that it had been him, he'd lose the opportunity to have her love him. To choose him. But to not tell her that it was him in her bed that night, not Andrew, railed at his conscience.

"The duke offered for my hand when he caught me distracted in the music room and I said yes without a moment's hesitation or emotion. I understand if this information is too much for you to bear, and if you wish to remove yourself from my life."

Byron shook his head, tipping up her jaw so she would look at him. The unshed tears that he saw swelling in her eyes broke his heart. He was a bastard to have done this to her. But no matter how much he wanted to tell her the truth, the words would not form. She would not forgive him should he say he'd thought she'd come to his room for him. That she'd finally realized the friendship they had was also a romantic one. The idea that she would not believe that Andrew had tricked them both and that he would lose her because of it made his throat tighten in fear. Selfish as it was, he could not lose her now, not when he'd only just won the woman he'd always adored.

"This does not make me think any less of you. To have

married the duke, to have sacrificed yourself to a man you did not love, makes you honorable." Something that Byron had not done. If he could go back he would've fought for her, told her the truth of that night. Outed his brother for the instigator he was. But they could not go back, they could only go forward. "You are to be commended, nothing else."

She searched his gaze, her eyes brightening with hope. "You do not hate me."

"I could never hate you, Nina. Ever."

She nodded, reaching out and clasping his hand just as the door opened and a footman came in carrying a tray of tea along with some steaming freshly baked scones.

Nina waited for the footman to leave before she said, "Thank you, Byron. I do not know what I would do without you. You're so very understanding toward me, especially since I ruined myself with your brother and now I'm wanting to ruin myself with you."

His body had a visceral reaction to her words and he wanted to haul her onto his lap and kiss her senseless. "You're not ruined," he said, tugging her over to him. She came willingly and he stared at her a moment, basking in her beauty before he leaned down and kissed her.

The touch fired his blood. Nina clasped his face, kissing him back with a need that matched his own. After wanting her for so long, he wasn't certain that they could come away from this embrace without going further. And he wanted to go further, so much further.

Nina broke the kiss and straddled his legs, her gown pooling at her waist. The warmth of her body rocked against his as she kissed him again. He wanted to love her again. Had longed for and dreamed of such a moment for years. To have her want him, not his brother, but him, left him breathless. He needed to hear his name on her lips.

She moaned as he pushed her against his sex, teasing them both. "Please tell me you're not going to scuttle away this time and leave me desperate for your touch for another day. I do not think I could bear that again."

He chuckled, rubbing her against him again. "You enjoyed our time in the carriage, I take it. Did you like the touch of my mouth on your breast, suckling you, teasing you with my tongue?"

She closed her eyes, her sex pressed hard against his and making his control waver. No one would be scuttling anywhere. If anything, he would take Nina here and now, on the settee, and be damned anyone who interrupted them.

"Yes," she gasped through their kiss. "I want you, Byron. Here. Now."

Her words lit a fire in his blood and he reached down between them, all pretence of restraint, of taking his time to savor the deliciousness of her gone. He ripped his frontfalls open, and opening her pantalets, he guided her onto his cock.

She stretched over him, then slowly sank down until she took his full length, and he groaned. Her warmth wrapped tight about his member and he took a calming breath, not wanting to lose control of himself like a green, untried lad.

Her hands spiked into his hair and she clasped him tight, and with slow, delicious torture she lifted herself a little before lowering herself once again.

This time she gasped out a sigh of pleasure and he held tightly against her hips, trying in some way to gain control of not only her movements but his as well.

"You're so beautiful," he said, kissing her soundly. Her tongue meshed with his and with each undulation, whispered sigh, and decadent kiss his control wavered on a cliff's edge.

"Oh, Byron." She held onto him tighter, her movements more frantic and deep. At this time he tried to deny himself his pleasure, wanting her to release first, to orgasm while fucking his cock. Just the thought of it made his balls ache and he reached to touch her mons, flicking her little nubbin as she rode him hard.

"Let go, Nina," he begged, the sound of his name on her lips, not anyone else's, making it impossible not to lose control. She was everything to him and he would do all that he could to ensure she enjoyed their time together, whether it be under intimate circumstances such as this, or when they were in company.

She kissed him hard and he moaned as she tightened about him, her climax strong and pulling him toward the same conclusion. He lasted as long as he could bear, before his balls tightened and he came hard and long into her heat.

She sank against his chest, their breathing rapid as they both came back to reality. Thankfully no one had entered while they were engaged in the middle of the afternoon with such acts. He ran a hand over Nina's back, simply touching her, reveling in the fact that she was in his arms finally.

"Nina," he said, waiting for her to look at him. She released a contented sigh and lay her head on his shoulder, staring up at him.

"Yes," she said lazily.

He watched her for a moment, emotions swelling up

inside him so much so that he could no longer hold them back. "I love you. I've always loved you."

Her eyes widened and she sat up, looking at him as if he'd grown two heads. He grinned. "You're shocked, I can see."

"Well," she mumbled, "I am, yes. We've been friends for so long and, well, I have always loved you too."

"Not in that way." He shook his head, clasping her face in his hands. "I love you as a man loves a woman. As a husband ought to love his wife. I love you so much more than a friend loves another friend."

He didn't expect her to say it back to him. In time he hoped that she would, but no longer could he go on without telling her how he felt. He'd made many mistakes when it came to them, but he would try and go forward without any. That would also include telling her the truth of them all those years ago. It was time Nina knew the truth, and he could only hope to God that she would give him the chance to atone for his hand in his brother's scheme. Forgive him his part of the sin.

NINA CLASPED BYRON'S CHEEKS, WISHING SHE COULD TELL HIM that she loved him too, but she could not, when she'd only told him half the story. To admit to marrying the duke out of spite was one thing, but then to allow her husband to believe the children in her belly were his was a shame she could not bear to voice aloud.

Byron may love her, and she adored him in return, but to keep the truth from someone, to not allow Byron's brother the opportunity to know his children, even if from afar, was a shame she carried with her every day. There was no certainty that Byron would forgive such duplicity, even if she and Andrew had done wrong by each other all those years ago. To hear such truths now would ruin what they'd just shared, and selfishly, she didn't want to have that conversation now. In time she would, just not yet.

She wiggled off Byron's lap and set her gown to rights, watching him out of the corner of her eye as he did the same with his buckskins. He stood, so tall and strong, with his chiseled jaw and his dark, intense eyes staring at her and making her stomach twist in delightful knots.

"Dine with me tomorrow night," he said. "Alone, just the two of us. I want you to myself."

"Where will we dine? You're staying at your family home in London, where I'm sure I need not remind you that your brother and his wife are also staying."

He placed a stray piece of her hair behind her ear and sighed. "They're out that evening, and will not be back until the early hours of the morning. Come to dinner," he persisted, throwing her a glance that was pure imploring. "I shall have Cook bake up your favorite dishes."

Nina chuckled, stepping against him and wrapping her arms about his waist. How lovely that they could be like this. Tactile and open with their thoughts. And soon she would be open to him about her daughters. "Very well, I shall come. What time do you wish for me to arrive?"

"Eight will do perfectly," he said, kissing her softly. "Tomorrow. Eight." He stepped away and started toward the door. "Sharp."

She watched him go, then looked down at the little table before the settee realizing they'd not taken tea or eaten any of the scones that had been brought in. She rang the bell and ordered a bath. There were no entertainments that she was to attend this evening, which gave her time to think about when and how she would tell Byron the truth.

His reaction to knowing that Nina had slept with his brother had gone better than she'd thought. Some men would never forgive such a thing, but then, Byron had always been different. Open minded, caring toward her, as a best friend ought to be she supposed.

He'd always been her knight prior to the years that they had been parted. It should not come as any surprise to her that he would support and understand why she'd done what she had, and forgive her actions.

It gave her hope that he would forgive her keeping the fact the girls were Andrew's children from his brother. She left the parlor and started up the stairs, the sound of her daughters' laughter in their room bringing a smile to her lips.

She would hold onto the fact that Byron would accept her truth when she told it, and not fret about it now. Tomorrow she had a meeting with the London Relief Society and needed to get an early night. She checked in on the girls, wishing them goodnight before heading off to her own room.

Dinner tomorrow evening would be delightful with Byron, and her stomach fluttered with the knowledge she would see him again. He was the very best of men, and if her reactions toward him told her anything, she was falling in love with her best friend too. No, she wasn't falling in love with him. She had fallen in love.

CHAPTER
ELEVEN

Byron sat in the library and watched as the clock ticked slowly toward the hour Nina was to arrive. He downed his brandy, running a hand through his hair. His brother, damn the man and his meddling wife, were running late and had not yet left for their evening engagement.

At this stage there was a chance they would all cross paths in the hall. The knocker sounded and Byron swore, standing and adjusting his cravat he headed out to the entrance to greet Nina.

She came into the house, untying her cloak and handing it to a waiting footman. Byron's step halted and for a moment his ability to speak evaded him. She threw him a knowing smile, before stretching out her hand for him to kiss.

"Good evening, Mr. Hill. I hope I'm not late for our dinner."

He shook his head, lifting her hand, but instead of kissing the back of her glove, he turned her hand over and kissed her palm. She took the opportunity to touch his cheek, before he wrapped her arm around his and started toward the dining room.

"Dinner will be served directly, so I thought we'd skip pre-dinner drinks and proceed straight in to dine."

"Are you eager for dessert, Mr. Hill?" she asked, grinning mischievously up at him.

Oh hell yes, he was eager. And once the dinner was served, he had full intentions of dismissing the staff and having her alone for the remainder of the meal.

"Your Grace?"

Nina halted at the dining room door and turned startled eyes up toward his brother, who stood at the top of the stairs.

"I did not know Byron was having company tonight, ah..." Andrew gestured with his hands, "with you. I did not think you would ever grace our home again."

Nina raised her chin, and the cool glance she bestowed on his brother would be enough to halt any ideas of friendship, if that was what he was aiming for. "Byron and I were friends long before I set my sights on you, Andrew."

Byron bit back a laugh at his brother's shocked countenance, but he stilled when Fionna came to stand beside her husband, taking his arm and walking down the stairs.

"Let us leave them, Andrew. It seems the rumors about the duchess are true."

Byron covered Nina's hand on his arm with his own. She'd always had a quick temper, and on hearing such slander he doubted she'd allow the slight to stand. "You owe the duchess an apology, Fionna. You know as well as Andrew that we've been friends for many years. Our dinner this evening is nothing but a dinner between friends."

Nina chuckled, looking up at Andrew and his wife. "They would not know what friends are, Byron. Just as rumors circulate about me, they circulate about you too, Mr. and Mrs. Hill. And let me tell you that you're known as the most boring couple in London this Season. Maybe you should refrain from insulting your betters and try to have a little fun before you return to Ireland. In fact," Nina continued, stepping away from Byron and heading toward the dining room. "I don't believe I've ever seen either of you smile. Some would think you do not like each other very much."

"Edwina, how can you be so cutting?" Andrew demanded, taking his wife's arm and assisting her down the remainder of the stairs.

Nina shrugged. "I speak as I find. Good evening," she said, walking into the dining room.

Byron glared at his brother, who glowered back. He sighed when the front door slammed shut. Taking a deep breath, he joined Nina. After having the servants bring in the three courses, he dismissed them for the evening.

"I apologize, Nina. I thought they would have been gone by eight. Had I known I would've sent word to halt your arrival."

She shook her head a little, spooning out a bowl of turtle soup for herself. "While I'm sad that we obviously cannot be civil to one another and at least pretend to get along, I can understand her hatred of me. I'm sure Andrew told her that he once courted me."

Byron nodded, but even to him it was noncommittal. His brother had told Fionna that he had courted Nina, but not that she'd propositioned him, and that her husband had agreed to the proposition, only then to trick Byron into swapping rooms with him, allowing Nina to turn up at his suite thinking he was Andrew.

What a wicked mess they'd all made of their lives, the lies that they lived with and tried to keep from one another.

"Let us not talk of them any longer. I understand you had a meeting today with the London Relief Society. How did that go? Have you made any more progress on your school?" he asked, giving Nina his full attention.

"The meeting went well. We're thinking that some of the older children—those who wish to learn how to work in stables or around horses, or do farm work—could start schooling in Kent with me. A program of sorts to have the children move out of the city to pursue another line of work if they liked. Of course we'd still have the learning of numbers and letters, but we also need to look at schooling as a pathway into their future. A stepping stone that will lead them in a direction of secure employment, away from the vicious and sometimes nasty temptations of London life."

Byron watched her mouth as she spoke about the children she would help, her ideas and dreams for her school. An overwhelming sense of respect and pure adoration thrummed through him. How could she be so wonderful? How lucky he was to have been given a second chance with her.

Their dinner came to an end, and she sipped her port, watching him over her glass. "You're very quiet, Mr. Hill. Have I talked you mute? I know I've been very vocal in my ideas. I hope I haven't bored you this evening."

He chuckled, placing down his own glass of port. "You've not bored me. On the contrary. If anything, you inspire me to do better." And he would, if she would let him help. He'd marry her tomorrow and follow her to the ends of the earth helping as many people as she wished, if only she'd say yes to being his wife.

"You shouldn't say such things. I may take you up on your newfound inspiration and have you help me."

"Merely name what you wish and I shall follow your command."

"Really?" She grinned mischievously. "So," she said, pushing back her chair to come and stand before him. "If I were to ask you to take me to your room, lay me down on your bed and make love to me, you would?"

Every cell in Byron's body hardened at the thought and he swallowed. He reached out and ran his hand over her hip, the silk of her gown no impediment, allowing him to feel every curve of her perfect form.

"I would." He met her gaze and she stepped between his legs, running her hand into his hair, fisting it a little. "I would do anything for you, Nina."

Her fingers tightened as she leaned down and kissed him. He'd thought the kiss would be full of fire, hunger, all the things he was feeling right at this time for her, but instead, it was slow, an exploration and sweet seduction that had he been standing would've brought him to his knees.

He stood and swooped her up into his arms, smiling at her little squeal of laughter, before leaving the dining room and heading for his bedchamber.

"I don't believe I've ever seen your bedroom before, Mr. Hill. How very scandalous of you to carry a woman who you've had over to dine up to your bedroom. What will the servants have to say about this?"

"I don't give a damn what anyone has to say." And luckily enough, to prove his point they passed two footmen on the upstairs landing, their widened eyes proof that he would have to offer for Nina, and soon. Not that he'd not intended to do exactly that. In fact, now that he had her here, it was the perfect time to ask her to be his always.

One of the footmen scrambled to open his bedchamber door, and thanking the servant he kicked it shut with his foot, placing Nina on his bed. Then he went back over to the door and snipped the lock before turning to watch her.

"Undress, Duchess," he said, pulling his cravat from around his neck. He stayed by the door, content to watch as she reached behind her back and started removing her gown. He divested himself of his clothing, strolling slowly toward the bed as he watched her slip the gown over one shoulder then the next before wiggling out of it on his bed.

Her sheer shift allowed him to see her bountiful breasts and the darkened tone of her erect nipples that poked outwards and all but begged him to kiss them. And before this night was over he would kiss them, and every inch of her body.

"And now the shift, Duchess. I want you naked and I want to see you strip before me."

She raised her brow, and he wondered if she'd take a dislike to his orders, but instead of disobeying, she reached for the ties at her neck and pulled them loose, allowing the shift to gape at her front. Just as she did with her gown, she slid it off one shoulder and the next before it too pooled at her legs on the bed. "The correct term is dowager duchess, just so you know."

Byron ignored her jibe, too taken by having her fully naked before him. Not since the day they had slept together all those years ago had he seen her such. He'd often tried to imagine the sight in his mind over the years, and sometimes he'd been successful in remembering, but nothing was as wonderful as seeing Nina in the flesh, her bountiful body his to love, his to adore.

He walked to the bed, reached out and ran a finger down the middle of her chest. Slowly he traced the soft skin on her stomach, before letting it slide to touch her navel. "You're so beautiful. You make my heart hurt."

She shivered and he stepped closer still, smelling the jasmine scent she washed her hair with always, the clean scent of lavender soap on her skin.

"You make mine hurt as well."

He kissed her, slowly lowering her to the bed and settling between her thighs. She kissed him with such tenderness that he thought he may die of happiness. For the love of her.

───────

NINA LET GO OF ANY INHIBITIONS OR CONCERNS ABOUT WHAT anyone would think of their relationship and simply enjoyed having Byron above her, kissing her, stroking her with the sweetest, lightest touches that drove her insane with need.

She wanted him with an intensity that scared her, and wrapping her legs about his waist, she urged him to have her. Inch by delicious inch he slid into her, filling and inflaming her more than he ever had before. Something had changed between them. Somewhere between their love for each other as friends it had blossomed into lust and soul-changing love.

Nina met his eyes as he pushed into her, clasping his face to pull him down for a kiss. "I love you too, Byron," she said, moaning as he flexed his hips and shot a bolt of pleasure through her core.

He continued to tease her with slow, agonisingly good strokes, each one teasing, tempting her a little closer to release. He was a wicked, wonderful man, and her heart burst with affection for him. She would make him marry her if it were the last thing she did before returning home at the end of the Season.

Byron was hers and she was his and there was little anyone or anything could do about it.

He lifted her hips, changing the angle to their lovemaking, and she cried out his name as wave after wave of pleasure rocked from her core to every part of her body. Byron's release followed and they crumpled into a heap of arms and legs, content to remain joined, but simply lying beside one another, lightly stroking, sleeping when they wished.

"Nina, you've been my friend for so long. These past weeks have been the happiest of my life and I want it to continue." He pushed her hair away from her face, placing it over her shoulder. He stared at her a moment, and she had an inkling where this conversation was headed.

She lifted herself to lay over his chest, to see him better. "I know, it's been the same for me too."

His thumb ran down her cheek and across her bottom lip. "Marry me."

She grinned, unable to hide her delight at his question, and why would she want to? She loved him as well. Wanted him as her husband for now and always. It may not have been her plan when coming to London this Season, but plans change, and so too would her life, for there was little chance she'd ever say no.

"Yes," she said, smiling through the flood of tears that threatened. "Yes, I will marry you, my beautiful, wonderful friend."

Byron rolled her over onto her back and she chuckled at his delight. "I'm going to spoil you and your girls for the remainder of my life."

A lump formed in her throat at his sweet words regarding their future and that of her girls. "Call on me tomorrow evening and we'll dine again, but this time with the girls and give them the news. If you could arrive a little before dinner, say six, there are a few things I want to discuss with you."

"Nothing serious, I hope," he said, kissing her gently.

Nerves pooled in Nina's stomach and she shook her head, hoping against hope that what she would tell him about her daughters wouldn't end with him rescinding his offer of marriage.

"No, nothing terrible I assure you. Simply legalities regarding our forthcoming marriage."

"Very well, I shall see you then. Now," he said, rolling onto his back and pulling her into the crook of his arm. "Tell me everything that I missed while I was away. I want to know everything about you and your daughters before we tell them the news tomorrow."

Nina threw herself into the conversation, only too happy to change the subject of what she would have to disclose the following night. She pushed away her nerves at the thought that Byron may not be able to stomach the fact his future stepdaughters were also his nieces. She reminded herself that his love for her, their history as friends, would make him forgive her, see that it wasn't entirely her fault or something that was planned. That it was simply the result of her hasty decision to throw herself at a gentleman when she was a young and foolish debutante.

BEFORE DAWN, NINA WROTE A NOTE TO BYRON AND LEFT IT ON HIS pillow, before dressing and sneaking downstairs to leave. A footman stood at the front door, even at this early hour when she'd hoped no one would be up.

"Can I help you with anything, Your Grace?" he asked, opening the door.

"Would you hail a hackney for me, please?"

She waited inside while the footman went to fetch her a cab, and a moving shadow in the corner of her vision almost gave her a heart seizure before she realized it was Andrew standing at the library door threshold.

"May I have a word, Your Grace," he said, turning to walk back into the room.

The footman came inside and she asked him to hold the cab for her before going into the library and closing the door. This was the first time she'd been alone with Andrew since the night they'd spent together. She was pleased to find that being before him, alone and in a shadowed room, she didn't feel one titbit of emotion toward him, except for disappointment. He was no gentleman in her book and hadn't been for many years now.

"Sneaking out, are we?" he said, raising his brow.

With him standing before the lit hearth, she could see the slight shadow of stubble on his jaw and his mussed hair. He still looked to be wearing the same clothing from the night before and she wondered why he wasn't upstairs, with his wife.

"What do you want, Andrew?" she asked, her words blunt and without any niceties, because of course he deserved none.

"I don't want anything from you, but I can assume that for you to still be here at this early hour of the day, you and my brother must be courting. That you've forgiven him his actions all those years ago and are willing to move forward together as a couple."

Nina frowned and narrowed her eyes at Andrew, trying to gauge if he were simply making trouble or if he was referring to something that she didn't know.

"We are engaged, not that it has anything to do with you. You lost the right to have any opinion in my life years ago. Not that I need to remind you of what kind of blaggard you are." The worst kind any young woman could have the displeasure of meeting.

He chuckled and her temper snapped. "You dare laugh at me, after what you did? I'm sure your wife doesn't know the truth of that night."

Andrew stared at her for a moment and then laughed harder. "And I can assume by your accusations that you do not know the truth either, my dear." He sighed, and not that she wanted to see it, but pity crossed his features before he said, "We never slept together, Nina. If you knew me at all, which you did not, you would know I wasn't capable of ruining an unmarried maiden without offering marriage. As much as I knew your feelings toward me were more than what I could offer you, I also knew my brother was infatuated with you and so I played a little trick on you both."

Dread formed like stone in her stomach and the room spun. She slumped onto a settee and fought to breathe. "Are you telling me that it was Byron who I slept with all those years ago and not you? How could you do that to me? You knew how I felt about you."

He shook his head, coming to sit at her side. His breath reeked of spirits and she shuffled away a little so as not to smell him. "I knew you were in love with me, or at least what you thought love was at that time, and no matter how many times I tried to dissuade you, you never got the hint. And so I found an alternative solution." He chuckled and she swallowed the bile that rose in her throat. "The look on my brother's face the following morning when he found you engaged to the duke was a moment I'll never forget. I knew my plan had been successful, that you had acted the whore and bedded him, and then you broke his heart. How sad for you both."

"But that means..." Nina's stomach lurched and she clasped her chest. "Oh dear lord. That means..."

"What does it mean?" he asked, flicking a piece of invisible lint from his rumpled coat.

"All these years I'd thought it was you. That you had slept with me to only turn around the next day and offer for someone else. But it wasn't you. Your brother, he didn't tell me it was him instead of you." Nina couldn't get the words out, so lodged were they in her throat. Had she called out Andrew's name that night? That she couldn't remember, but if she had, Byron had not corrected her on it. How could she ever forgive such duplicity? "You bastard. You swine. How could you do that to me, or to your sibling for that matter? Do you have no conscience at all?"

Andrew sighed, staring at the fire. "I suppose I do not, but it has all worked out well in the end. You're engaged, as you said. No harm done."

No harm done! The man was mad.

"Since my arrival in town I've been beseeching Byron to tell you the truth," he continued. "I knew you loathed me, and that has caused tension between my wife and myself. She suspects you're angry with me for something, but she doesn't know what. I don't want her to hear the false statement from you that it was I who took your virtue, when it was not. But Byron has not done what I wanted him to do, even though he's had multiple opportunities to do so."

Nina fought not to cast up her accounts. Byron was the

father of her children. Did he suspect? He would be a simpleton indeed if he'd not at least had the thought once. She certainly would have, had she been in Byron's shoes.

"After this day, we will never speak again. Had you done the right thing all those years ago and told me that you loved another, I would've been hurt, yes, but I would've moved on, just as many young debutantes do every day. Your hand in this is just as prevalent as your brother's, and I'll never forgive either of you."

She stood, swiping at her cheek and hating the fact she was crying in front of a man whom she really wanted to hit.

Andrew stood, swaying a little. "Had I had the inclination I should've stepped aside years ago when I knew that Byron adored you, but I did not. I liked the attention, you see. A young foolish pup wanting to rub it in my brother's face that I too could woo women, take what I wanted. That Season was jolly good fun, you must admit."

Nina started for the door, the pain of the truth ripping her in two. Byron had seduced her under false pretences. Friends to the very last did not do such things to one another. The memory of that night, of what they had done...how he had kissed every inch of her body, kissed her in places she'd not known possible. She cringed at the horror of it all. Oh dear God, she would never forgive him. How could he break her trust in such a manner? People who love one another, as Byron stated he did her, did not do such things.

She wrenched the door open and started for the entrance, the bang of the door as it hit the wall inside the parlor loud in the early hours.

"Nina?"

Byron's voice at the top of the stairs only made her stride faster. Not waiting for the footman, she ran for the carriage that waited outside. She heard Byron call out her name, the sound of his footsteps audible even from outside. "Berkley Square, and hurry." She climbed up into the carriage, settling back into the seat and not looking back at the house as the carriage pulled away at a clipping speed.

She would confront Byron—there was no doubt that such a conversation would need to be had—but she needed time to think through what she would do. How she would handle knowing a truth that changed so many things in her life. Who she loved, who she trusted, who her children's father was.

A sob escaped and she clasped a hand over her mouth to try to calm herself. How could the brothers have done such a thing to her? It was truly the cruellest trick anyone could ever play, and to think her best friend, the man she loved, could deceive her in such a way made it even more so.

CHAPTER

TWELVE

No sooner had Nina arrived home than the sound of banging on the front door alerted her to the fact that Byron had followed her there. She went into her study, pouring herself a good drum of brandy, and noted the time. It was still very early, and the girls wouldn't be up for some hours. Perhaps it was best she tell Byron what she thought of his duplicity now, while she was still seething and hurt from the news.

After they parted this day, she would return to Kent and forget she'd ever been fooled by the Hill brothers. Andrew said he'd played a trick on both her and Byron, but was that so? Or did Byron realize early on in her arrival to his room that night that she was there for Andrew and take advantage of the fact? The sound of mumbling in the hall filtered to her, followed by determined footsteps upon the parquetry floor.

The door to the study opened and Byron came in, closing it behind him just as quickly. He held out his hand, in supplication she supposed, but it did little to cool her temper.

124

"Nina, let me explain. Please, my love," he said, coming to take her hand.

She slapped his arm away, going over near the desk to put space between them. "Explain then. Explain to me how you slept with me all those years ago, allowed me to believe you were Andrew, when all the time you knew that it was you in my bed. That I had given myself to the wrong brother."

His shoulders slumped and she fought the little shred of remorse she felt for him.

"I have no excuse, there is none. But please know I had no idea you would ever come to my room. I didn't know that you had propositioned my brother. He merely asked me to swap rooms due to the bed being too hard, otherwise I would not have been there. I'd loved you from afar for so long, I thought you being in my room meant you'd finally seen my worth. I thought you were there for me." He paced on the opposite side of the chaise lounge, his hands gesturing with each word. "I couldn't believe my turn of luck. That you were before me, offering to love me, and I could no sooner turn away air." He shook his head, seemingly lost to the past. "When I saw the hope, the desire in your eyes, I truly believed it was for me. So I gave you what you wanted."

"What I wanted? I never wanted to be tricked! I never wanted you."

He cringed and she hated she had to hurt him, but the lie that she'd not been privy to pushed her remorse aside. "Nina, please, I loved you even then. I've wanted to tell you for so long, but how do you tell someone such a thing? It was not our fault it happened, it was Andrew's."

She glared at him, wishing him anywhere but here. "You didn't have to deceive me. You could've declared your feelings toward me years ago. Andrew may have tricked me into going to your room, but surely you must have known that my character wasn't fickle. That I truly thought myself in love with your brother. That I wouldn't change my mind overnight and throw myself at your head."

He shook his head, dejected. "I was blinded by hope. I thought finally you had turned your sights onto me. I was mistaken."

Her temper soared, and she fisted her hands at her side. "The difference between you and me, Byron, is that I was honest. I went to the room thinking it was Andrew's chamber. The following morning you realized your mistake and still you kept the truth from me. Do not try to fool me into thinking you're innocent in this. That it was a silly error that we should all move on from."

"I wish it were so simple, but I have no excuse and you know that. I adore you, I've loved you for years. I hated that you only saw my brother and not me." He gestured to his chest and she swallowed the tears that threatened to run unheeded down her face. "But you never did. You only saw perfect, placid Andrew. I knew the mistake we'd both made when you left me that night—if you remember, you whispered Andrew's name in my ear." He placed his hand on his heart. "I swear, until that moment I thought you were there for me. By the time I realized your mistake, it was too late. I planned to court you after that, thought through the rest of the night how I would make you mine, seduce you if I had to, but you accepted the Duke of Exeter's proposal and I never had a chance."

She turned her back on him, her blood hot with anger and pain. "You have no idea what you've done." Her voice cracked and she heard him start toward her, but she moved out of his reach.

"I know what I've done, but surely nothing was so lost that we cannot move forward with this. I want a life with you, Nina. I want to be there for you and your girls. I want to help you with your school. Let me. Forgive me, please," he begged.

"I cannot." She shook her head, unable to voice the words she must. She sniffed, wanting to flee but knowing she could not. "I have not told you everything. There is more to this sorry tale that you and your wicked brother do not know."

BYRON FROWNED, UNSURE OF WHAT SHE SPOKE. "WHAT DO YOU mean? What is it that I do not know?"

Nina clasped her hands before her and took a calming breath. "I loathed your brother for so many years, not simply because I believed he took my virtue like a thief in the night and then up and married someone else. Although that is a good enough reason to loathe him, it wasn't what drove my hate for so long."

"Then what was?" he asked, detesting the fact that he'd done this to her. What a selfish bastard he was.

"I accepted the duke out of sheer fury at your brother's choice, and the fact that my parents had been pushing for a grand match. I figured if I could not have the man I loved, I would therefore marry for money and status. Elevate myself to be higher than Andrew in society and therefore crush him if I chose whenever he dared show his face in London. But I forgot all of that the moment I found out I was with child. A child—two children—I believed to be Andrew's, but which I now know are yours. The girls are not the duke's or Andrew's children. They are yours, Byron."

He stared at her as her unrepentant loathing of his sibling came into focus. Now it made sense why she'd hated Andrew for so long, years after the fact. Byron thought about the girls, remembered their features, and wondered how he'd not noticed before that they both had his eyes, his dark locks. How they looked nothing like the Duke of Exeter.

The girls were five. He'd missed five years of their lives. A cold annoyance settled in his gut at the realization. "You kept them from me or from Andrew or whoever," he said, more harshly than he ought. He ran a hand through his hair, unable to believe what he was hearing. He was a father. He had two daughters, the sweetest little cherubs, and he didn't know them. At all. "Why did you have to run off and marry the duke like the devil himself was after you? I went looking for you the next day only to find betrothal celebrations happening for both you and Andrew. I didn't have time to court you, to make you see me, for you were already another's."

She stormed over to him, standing as tall as she could before him, which wasn't very high considering he stood a good head above her. "How dare you even say such things! Do not forget I did not know it was you in my bed, not your brother. Count yourself fortunate that I did marry the duke, for he thought the girls were his and he gave them legitimacy. If I had waited I would have been ruined."

"You were ruined the moment you sent a missive to my brother asking him to sleep with you."

She reeled away from him and he went to her, wanting to pull her into his arms and hold her close. Damn it. "I'm sorry, Nina. I didn't mean that."

"Get out," she said, pushing him away. "I don't want to see you. I don't want to know you. I don't want anything to do with you, now or ever."

Panic rose in his gut and he swore. "I will not lose you now. I will not lose my girls."

"You never had us. To society at large they are the deceased Duke of Exeter's children and they will always be known as such."

She shouted for the footman and he entered within a moment. "Escort Mr. Hill outside, Carter, and fetch Digby if he causes you any trouble."

She turned her back on him and Byron watched her for a moment, collecting his thoughts before he did as she bade. He would give her time. Hell, he needed time to think through what had been said this morning.

"I will call on you tomorrow and we will discuss this further when we're both calmer. Good day, Your Grace."

He left her then, striding out onto Berkley Square and fighting to remain calm. A groomsman held his horse and he thanked him before climbing up. Everything would be well. He would give her time and he would calm down and then he could go about setting things to right.

Whatever that right may be.

CHAPTER

THIRTEEN

Nina pushed her horse hard into a gallop across
the fields of her Scottish estate, the wind whip-
ping at her hair that had long fallen out of its
pinned style.

The day Byron had called on her, a month ago now,
she'd packed up the house in Berkley Square and left
London. They had travelled at a blistering speed away from
town and arrived at Lengrove Hall within a week. Here in
Scotland, the home that she had inherited from her
paternal grandmother was her safe house. Here she could
live free from the ridicule of the *ton*, of seeing her friends
look at her with pity once they knew that she and Byron
would not be marrying. They didn't need to be privy to the
sad details, but it still would not stop them from hovering
with concern, something she did not want to endure. Not
ever.

She was the worst of people. In a way Byron had been
right—she had caused a lot of her problems herself. It was
certainly she who had asked Andrew to sleep with her to
begin with. Byron had been a pawn in his brother's sick

game as much as she was, and she hated to remember what she'd said to him.

But Byron should've told her as soon as he found out the truth of that night. In her anger she'd not asked when he'd been told of his brother's scheme, and it made her wonder if he'd only recently found out himself.

The weeks away from London had given her time to think about what might have happened if she hadn't reacted with such impulsiveness and accepted the duke's offer. What if she had gone to Byron and confessed all to her friend? Would he have shared his part in their sad tale, and thus the outcome might be different today? A terrible ache rose in her heart. He had left a pain so fierce that she wasn't sure she would ever be able to forgive him, or what had been done to them both.

She looked over her lands, wondering what Byron was doing right at this moment. Not even the current Duke of Exeter knew of this estate that her grandmother had owned, and until she returned to town, Byron would never find her here. This home had always had a feeling of safety, been a place where one could heal if they needed. And she so needed it now.

As angry and disillusioned as she was with Byron, she couldn't wedge the pesky emotion of love from her heart. Even after all he'd done to her, and she to him, she loved him. Every moment of every day since she'd been parted from his side she'd thought of him. Was he even thinking of her in return?

Nina pulled her gelding to a slow walk as she started into a glen, the mountains on either side of her making the air cooler than on the open ground. She would have to return to Kent soon. Only today a letter had arrived from her foreman there, saying that the building works had commenced and a new roof would be up within a month or so.

She had hoped Byron would've wanted to be part of her new life, her new direction, but it wasn't to be. His silence over the past month had been deafening, not even a missive. Her housekeeper in London knew her locale, and any correspondence would be forwarded to her here, but nothing had arrived and she could only think of one reason for his silence. And it wasn't a reason she wanted to acknowledge.

In the weeks that they'd been apart, Nina had thought over what had happened all those years ago, and the fact that she'd not been fair. Byron's brother had fooled them both, and although Byron had kept that truth from her, it wasn't his fault.

The thought that Andrew Hill and his scheming had resulted in the loss of her best friend, her lover, her future with Byron, was not a welcome one.

It had taken Byron days to get Nina's whereabouts out of Mrs. Widdle, her housekeeper in London. On his arrival at her home after their heartbreaking quarrel he'd been turned away with no explanation other than that the duchess had shut up the London property and left town.

He'd travelled to Kent only to find Granville Hall also vacant of its mistress. Unsure where to go to next, he'd ridden back to London, and after a lot of coaxing and downright bribery toward Mrs. Widdle, he'd managed to get Nina's address in Scotland.

That she'd travelled to Scotland with the children had come as a surprise. He didn't even know she had property there, not to mention the fact she'd moved so very far away from him didn't give him much hope that she would be willing to hear him out. To listen and let him explain what a complete and utter cod he'd been.

I'm so sorry, my darling...

Now he looked out the carriage window at the passing landscape. They were getting up into the highlands now, the mountains higher and some peaks with snow glistening on their tops. The driver had assured him it wasn't too much longer and he itched to see Nina again. It had been the longest month of his life.

He cringed as he recalled what he'd said to her. He looked up toward the heavens and prayed to the Almighty that she would forgive him his stupidity. He couldn't lose her. No matter what either of them had done, he loved her and he was sure she loved him in return.

The carriage came out of a darkened forest and he glimpsed the roof of a large Georgian home nestled at the base of a small hill, sitting before a fast-moving river.

The home was well cared for, and as night was almost upon them, some lights shone from the windows. Nerves pooled in his gut at the thought of seeing Nina again. It had been a month. Would she still be angry with him? Would she send him away?

The carriage made its way down the hill and pulled up before the house's double doors that faced the gravel drive. A footman opened the door, and Byron caught a glimpse of the inside of the home, a grand central staircase and a flash of children as they ran up it in haste, as if they were playing a game of chasey or hide and seek.

He stepped down and made his way to the door, and heard Nina yelling out to the girls that she would be up with them shortly. He stood at the threshold, not wanting to interrupt the family moment, but also wanting so desperately to be part of it. He wanted to be beside Nina when she sent the girls upstairs to dress or to get ready for bed with their nurse. He wanted to be their father in the truest sense, not just the man who created them during one night of passion.

He stepped inside, and before the footman had a chance to introduce him, Nina saw him, halting mid step as she headed toward the staircase, a book of some kind in her hand.

"What are you doing here?" she asked.

He couldn't read her features or work out what she was thinking, and he desperately wanted to know what was going on in that intelligent, beautiful mind of hers. He came to stand before her, wanting to touch her, but he refrained. There was time for that, when she'd forgiven him. "You're a hard woman to find."

"That's probably because I didn't want to be found." She turned and headed back toward the room she'd come from and he followed, shutting the door behind them. He watched as she went to stand in the centre of the large space, placing her book on a table that sat behind a three-seat settee.

He took in the room. It was a parlor or a games room, he wasn't sure which, but it had books, a desk, and a billiards table, along with an assortment of children's toys that sat in different spots about the room. It was very homely, and exuded a warm feel, just like Nina did toward those she loved. Not toward him so much at the moment.

"I've been trying to find you. It took some inducement to get your whereabouts out of your housekeeper, Mrs. Widdle, but as soon as I knew your location I came. We have to talk, Nina."

She sighed and gestured toward a chair before the hearth. He sat and a little piece of him died when she sat across from him and not beside him.

"Then talk."

Other than throwing himself at her feet, he wondered what else he could do to make her forgive him. Make her look at him again with love and respect. "I'm sorry. I'm sorry for everything. For loving you so much that I kept the painful truth of that night from you, when I knew you didn't know it was me. For not speaking out the next day and telling the world you would not be marrying the duke, but marrying me instead. I'm sorry for not being there when you carried our girls in your belly, when you gave birth to them, and while you cared for them these past years. I'm sorry for hurting you. You are the love of my life. I adore you, Nina. Please forgive me."

She sat back in her chair and glared at him. Her silence made panic claw at his throat and the option of throwing himself at her feet reared in his mind. It may work. It was certainly worth a try.

"You were my friend, Byron. I never saw you as anything other than that, and in my youthful foolishness I thought myself in love with your brother. I've done a lot of maturing since that night I threw myself at a man who did not want me. And over the last few weeks I've come to realize that perhaps you ending up as the man in my bed was fate playing its hand. Because what I feel for you is nothing like what I felt for your brother. What I feel for you is so much more. What I feel for you is true."

His heart burst with joy, and for the first time in a month he felt as though he could breathe. "Are you saying that you love me still? That there is a possibility for you and me, even with all the things we've hidden and done to one another?"

Nina stood and came to stand before him. She reached out a hand and pushed away the lock of hair that had fallen over his eye. "I am saying that. In fact," she said, sitting on his lap and wrapping her arm about his neck, "I want to make you and me permanent."

"So you'll marry me then?" he asked, grinning.

"Is this your way of asking me?" She raised her brow and he laughed. He supposed he could do a lot better than that when it came to proposing. But right now, he didn't want either of them to move. He wanted to stay exactly where they were.

"Marry me?" he asked, meeting her gaze and reveling in the love that shone back at him. A love that was solely for him and no one else.

She nodded. "I will marry you, Byron Hill, my oldest and dearest friend. And then we can raise our girls, and God willing our other children, together. No more wasted time. I don't want to spend another minute out of your company."

The idea sounded perfect to him as well. "Well, we're in Scotland. Perhaps a trip to Gretna is in order."

Nina chuckled. "I'll make arrangements and we'll leave tomorrow."

And they did.

EPILOGUE

12 months later

"Are you disappointed, Byron?" Nina asked, grinning at him over the stable door. "I know you were hoping for a boy," she said.

Byron looked down at his daughters dog Bentley, that had just become the proud father of five girl puppies. Not long after their marriage the girls had persuaded them to get another wolfhound—a female one—and now it would seem his destiny was to be surrounded by females of all species.

He patted Bentley, who sat at his side looking in on the makeshift bed that the girls had made the dogs in the barn. Not that they would be here for long. Soon all would be living indoors with them again. There was little that Byron wouldn't allow his daughters, and over the past twelve months they had successfully wrapped him about their little fingers and he was powerless against their charms. And the charms of his wife, who grinned over at him from the other side of the stable door.

"I'm not disappointed. You, my Nina, ought to stop your teasing."

She threw him a mischievous glance and his want of her increased. Hell, he loved her, so much more with every day that passed. They had married in Gretna within a week of his arrival in Scotland, and then returned to Kent to complete the building of Nina's school.

The past year had been the best of his life, and to know that his future held more of the same only increased his love of living.

"I think we'll call this one Bessie," Molly said, stroking the puppy on its ear with the lightest of strokes.

"You shouldn't touch the puppies," Lora said with authority. "They're only new and should be left alone." Lora threw her sister a knowing look, but Molly merely rolled her eyes.

"You are not an expert, Lora. Bentley and Bernadette don't mind me patting their babies and so you shouldn't either." Molly turned toward Nina. "Tell her, Mama Tell her that I'm right."

"I think, girls, it's time for lunch, so hurry up inside and clean up before we dine." Nina opened the stable door, and with begrudging moans the girls headed indoors. Byron also came out of the stall, pulling his wife up against his side before they followed the children.

He reached down and ran his hand over the small bump on Nina's stomach. "Maybe this will be a boy. Not that I care either way—you know I adore all my girls."

She smiled up at him, chuckling a little. "I know you do, but I would like a little boy, if only to replicate the wonderful man who'll be his father and role model."

"You're happy then?" he asked, kissing the top of her head and holding her close.

"The happiest. But then you already know that."

He did, for he was too. And when the time came, seven months later in fact, Nina did birth them another healthy child. A girl.

Dear Reader

Thank you for taking the time to read *To Dare a Duchess*! I hope you enjoyed the fifth book in my Lords of London series.

I'm forever grateful to my readers, so if you're able, I would appreciate an honest review of *To Dare a Duchess*. As they say, feed an author, leave a review! You can contact me at www.tamaragill.com to sign up to my newsletter to keep up with my writing news.

If you'd like to learn about book six in my Lords of London series, *To Marry a Marchioness*, please read on. I have included chapter one for your reading pleasure.

Tamara Gill

TO MARRY A MARCHIONESS

LORDS OF LONDON, BOOK 6

Lady Henrietta Zetland is definitely not looking for love again after being widowed so young. She cannot provide the heirs most husbands desire, so is quite happy to abandon the trappings of the ton and the London Season for country life. Yet the moment she meets Marcus Duncan, the new Marquess Zetland, the passion she has long suppressed returns to life and overwhelms all good sense and propriety.

Becoming a marquess is just what Marcus Duncan needs to save his crumbling Scottish estate. His travels to England to oversee his newly acquired estates throw him into the path of his cousin's widow. Marcus is instantly charmed by Henrietta, and when a passionate love affair ensues the last thing he expects is to lose his heart to her. Wanting more, he fears that the secret he's hiding will drive her away...but Henrietta has a secret of her own that could separate them forever.

CHAPTER

ONE

Lady Henrietta Nicholson, Marchioness of Zetland, sat before her bedroom dressing table and stared at her reflection. Her eyes were bloodshot and puffy, the tip of her nose was red, and her hair had somehow refused to be appropriate on this sombre day and stay confined under her hairpins.

Behind her, her maid bustled about the room, making her bed that now looked too large, empty, and cold, much like her life as she would know it from this day forward. Her mother, the Duchess of Athelby, was downstairs and not willing to leave Henrietta alone in this large estate that was now hers. The property had not been entailed, and she was free to live out the rest of her days in Surrey if she wished. How wonderful that idea sounded. Having laid her husband to rest in the cold, damp soil not an hour before, Henrietta needed something to look forward to.

She swiped at the tears that fell down her cheeks. How could this be her life? They had only been married twelve short months, it wasn't possible for Walter to be gone. His sickness had been so fast, a trifling cold that had settled in his lungs and then would not budge. No matter what they tried, or how many doctors they'd seen on Harley Street, his cough and his breathing steadily became worse until he passed in his sleep.

Henrietta thought back to the day she'd come upon him in their bedroom fighting for breath, and she'd known with sickening dread that he wasn't long for this earth. That the ailment that had wrought carnage on his body would win the war. Wanting to be strong for him, she'd not broken down until alone, and she had remained steadfast in her ability to remain calm in his presence, to try and keep him cheerful, when all the while her heart was crumbling in her chest knowing that he was slipping away. That she was going to lose him.

If only it had been a peaceful passing. His chest had rattled fiercely during the last hours and Henrietta had prepared herself as best she could. And now the worst was here and she was alone. The man she loved was no longer of this realm, and no matter how much her mother tried to comfort her, it was not her that Henrietta wanted at her side.

She sniffed and started to pull out what few pins she had left in her hair, placing them on the shallow crystal dish on her dressing table. Her mother wanted her to return to town with her, but Henrietta would stay in Surrey. This was her home now, the place she'd been happiest, and she wasn't willing to leave it only to be bombarded in town with pitying looks from friends and acquaintances, constant attempts to comfort and relay their sadness regarding her loss.

Her closest friends meant well, and she was thankful they'd come to Surrey to pay their last respects, but the social whirl of London no longer drew her like it once had.

Over the past year she'd become accustomed to country living, to running a large home of her own. The frivolities of London life seemed empty and silly now. The gossip and scandal. As much as she'd miss her friends, on the morrow she would bid them goodbye and selfishly be thankful for it.

Should she return to town the ton would expect her to marry again, and she would never do such a thing. She would not cheat another husband out of what they rightfully needed upon marriage—children. No, she was a widow. She would become a matron of the ton—if a very young one—when she eventually did return, and that would be her life.

A light knock sounded on the door and her maid opened it, revealing her mother. Even in middle age, the Duchess of Athelby was a beautiful woman. Many said that Henrietta took after her mama more than her dearest papa, but she'd always liked to think that she and her twin brother Henry took after them both.

"Are you alright, dearest? I thought I'd sleep in here with you this evening."

Henrietta smiled, taking in her mother in her nightgown and bare feet. Even if she'd wanted to be alone this evening, it was pointless to argue with her mama. If she thought she needed to stay, to give comfort—even if that comfort was without words—there was little Henrietta could say to persuade her otherwise.

"You may stay, Mama. I do not mind."

Her mother dismissed the maid and climbed up into the bed, arranging some pillows so she could sit upright.

"Have you given any thought to returning to London with me next week? Or perhaps even Ruxton estate? Your father thought it may be good for you to close up Kewell

Hall and come home for a while. Henry too. We discussed it this evening after you retired."

Did they just. Henrietta pushed away the flicker of annoyance that her family was arranging her, for they really only meant well. Today had been hard on them too, she reminded herself. They had loved Walter—there were few who did not—and they would miss him. "I have given it some thought," she said, standing and walking over to the bed, playing idly with the linens. "But I'm going to remain here, Mama. I promise I shall be fine," she continued when her mother looked at her with something akin to horror. "I will not do anything silly, but I want...no, I need, time to be alone. To come to terms with the fact that I'm a widow and Walter is gone. You understand, do you not? I shall return to town after my year of mourning, but until then, I want to be here. Near my horses, our pets, our garden and home. I just need to heal before I start running to where I'll never face the truth of my life." The truth being now that Walter was gone, she would be alone. Forever.

Her mama nodded, her eyes hooded with sadness. "You've been so strong throughout this whole ordeal, my dear. It is acceptable to break when we lose someone we love. Fortunately, you've never lost a loved one before, so I worry that you're bottling your emotions up."

Henrietta swallowed the lump in her throat. She had been strong, and now that she no longer needed to be, all she wished was to be alone. To crumble and break by herself so she may put the pieces of her life back together. She'd never been an impractical woman, but something told her she'd be anything but her usual self in the next few months.

"I love you so much, darling," her mama said. "If I could take away this pain, if I could turn back the clock and give you Walter back, I would in a heartbeat. I'll worry for you if you stay here. Maybe I could delay my departure. I'm sure your papa will not mind in the least."

Henrietta climbed up into bed beside her mama, lying down and cuddling into her arms. "I want you to go with Papa. I'm sad, and I shall cry just as we are now, but I shall be fine. In time. I promise I shall write to you every week, but I need to be on my own at present. I promise all will be well again." Henrietta hoped that was true. The estate and the people who depended on its success were relying on her to make it so. The new marquess would take care of Walter's other properties, but Kewell Hall was her responsibility and she would not fail these people. She would give herself a month at best to grieve and then she would have to rally and push herself into everyday duties. It was what Walter would want her to do. He loved her so very much that he'd never want her to wallow in unhappiness forever.

Her mother ran a hand through her hair, and Henrietta heard her sigh of defeat. "Very well, we shall return to town next week as planned. But I will visit every month or so. Surrey is not so far away, and for my own sanity you shall allow me to. I will never rest easy if I do not know that my baby girl is well."

Henrietta smiled, hugging her mama tighter. "I love you."

Her mother reached down and kissed her hair. "I love you too, my darling girl. And I promise you, your grief will lessen in time, and you'll find that life will carry on, even if you do not want it to. But it will, and when you're ready, you'll love again. You're too young, with too much of a beautiful soul, to be a widow forever."

The idea made Henrietta shudder. The thought of marrying again, of being intimate, of sharing any kind of life with someone who was not Walter was too abhorrent to imagine. She would never marry again, for the love of her life was gone, and such a love only came around once. No one was ever lucky enough to find two great loves in their life. Her mother ought to know very well how true that was, since Henrietta's father the Duke of Athelby was her mama's second marriage after her disastrous first one.

"You know as well as anyone that marriage will not happen again for me, Mama. I cannot marry a man knowing that I'm unable to bear children."

"The doctors could be wrong, dearest," her mother said.

Even to Henrietta her mother's tone held a sliver of despair. "A year of marriage and not one child, Mama. I think in my case they were correct, and I need to accept my fate. I will never be a mother." Not wanting to give her any more reason to worry, or to discuss the matter any further, she yawned, tiredness swamping her. "I need to sleep now, Mama."

"Very well." Her mother settled beside her. "Goodnight, darling."

"Goodnight, Mama." At least in sleep she might be oblivious to the pain that ricocheted through her with every breath. A pain that only sleep would relieve. A pain that she doubted would ever go away.

MARCUS DUNCAN SAT BEFORE THE ROARING FIRE IN HIS LIBRARY and read the missive notifying him that his distant cousin, the Marquess of Zetland, had passed away suddenly and unexpectedly from some sort of lung ailment.

He shook his head at the windfall that couldn't have happened at a better time. The knowledge that the marquessate was now his, along with all the properties that came with it, filled him with joy, as well as with despair for the late marquess's family. No one wished to come into lands, money, and a title in such a way, and he would write to them and support them in their grief.

It would also mean, ultimately, that he would have to travel from Scotland to England—leave his beloved son and homeland and deal with the legalities of the situation. Marcus looked down at Arthur, who was sitting with his nurse, playing with a wooden horse. Although his boy would not inherit the marquessate, or the unentailed lands and properties, his future would be more secure. The income Marcus would draw from the estates would help rebuild and repair his own here in Scotland, giving his son a solid footing for the future.

Guilt pricked his soul that he'd not been able to give that solid footing himself just by siring the boy. When one was born out of wedlock, the stigma followed like the waft of cow dung. But now that there was the possibility of fortune favouring them, well, that could change things a little for his lad, and that alone made him thankful.

He skimmed through the legal document that accompanied the letter from his solicitor in Edinburgh stating that his cousin's widow, the marchioness, had remained at Kewell Hall, but that there was some sort of trouble regarding who owned this unentailed estate and that further correspondence would be forthcoming.

Marcus supposed he would have to look over the estates, ensure all were in working order, and lease them out before he headed back to Scotland. His solicitor mentioned the possibility of leasing out the London townhouse as well, an income source that was timely due to the repairs required at his castle. Not that he had wished death upon his cousin, never that, but he would have to think in terms of his own financial responsibilities now that the marquisate was his.

Once the weather was better he would travel south, maybe in a month or two, but first he would have to go to Edinburgh to sign off on the inheritance and officially become the new Marquess of Zetland.

The name Zetland didn't roll off the tongue as well as Duncan did, but he'd never thought to inherit the title. His poor cousin. Dying at such a young age, and without heirs, must be a terrible blow to the family, and as much as they would hate anyone distant inheriting the seat, Marcus would do all that he could to help them with their grief. He may be a hard man, but he was not unkind.

He stood and went over to his desk, sitting down behind the four feet of mahogany. Sliding a piece of parchment closer, he scribbled a note to his solicitor that he would attend his office next week. As for when he'd leave for England, well, he would think of that later. With his own estate to take care of here in Scotland, and preparing for planting, he didn't have time right now to oversee the estates in England. His son needed him, and the windfall of inheriting the marquessate would give him some extra funds so work could commence on the east wing of his home. He couldn't very well leave now that he had an opportunity to complete all of the building repairs he'd longed to do. There were also numerous crofters homes that needed new roofing prior to winter, and other repairs that had only been temporary until his fortunes turned.

He would ensure the steward overseeing the marquess's homes started proceedings to lease out the properties to anyone who was interested, and have his solicitor forward any correspondence to him here. For the time being, this would be where he'd deal with any business at hand.

KISS THE WALLFLOWER SERIES AVAILABLE NOW!

If the roguish Lords of London are not for you and wallflowers are more your cup of tea, then below is the series for you. My Kiss the Wallflower series are linked through friendship and family in this four-book series. You can grab a copy on Amazon or read free through KindleUnlimited.

KISS THE WALLFLOWER

LEAGUE OF UNWEDDABLE GENTLEMEN SERIES AVAILABLE NOW!

Fall into my latest series, where the heroines have to fight for what they want, both regarding their life and love. And where the heroes may be unweddable to begin with, that is until they meet the women who'll change their fate. The League of Unweddable Gentlemen series is available now!

LEAGUE OF UNWEDDABLE GENTLEMEN

THE ROYAL HOUSE OF ATHARIA SERIES

If you love dashing dukes and want a royal adventure, make sure to check out my latest series, The Royal House of Atharia series! Book one, To Dream of You is available now at Amazon or you can read FREE with Kindle Unlimited.

ROYAL HOUSE OF ATHARIA

DON'T MISS TAMARA'S OTHER ROMANCE SERIES

Tempt Me, Your Grace

Hellion at Heart

Dare to be Scandalous

To Be Wicked With You

Kiss Me, Duke

The Marquess is Mine

Kiss the Wallflower

A Midsummer Kiss

A Kiss at Mistletoe

A Kiss in Spring

To Fall For a Kiss

A Duke's Wild Kiss

To Kiss a Highland Rose

Lords of London

To Bedevil a Duke

To Madden a Marquess

To Tempt an Earl

To Vex a Viscount

To Dare a Duchess

To Marry a Marchioness

To Marry a Rogue

Only an Earl Will Do

Only a Duke Will Do

Only a Viscount Will Do

Only a Marquess Will Do

Only a Lady Will Do

A Time Traveler's Highland Love

To Conquer a Scot

To Save a Savage Scot

To Win a Highland Scot

A Stolen Season

A Stolen Season

A Stolen Season: Bath

A Stolen Season: London

Scandalous London

A Gentleman's Promise

A Captain's Order

A Marriage Made in Mayfair

High Seas & High Stakes

His Lady Smuggler

Her Gentleman Pirate

A Wallflower's Christmas Wreath

Daughters Of The Gods

Banished

Guardian

Fallen

Stand Alone Books

Defiant Surrender

A Brazen Agreement

To Sin with Scandal

Outlaws

About the Author

Tamara is an Australian author who grew up in an old mining town in country South Australia, where her love of history was founded. So much so, she made her darling husband travel to the UK for their honeymoon, where she dragged him from one historical monument and castle to another.

A mother of three, her two little gentlemen in the making, a future lady (she hopes) keep her busy in the real world, but whenever she gets a moment's peace she loves to write romance novels in an array of genres, including regency, medieval and time travel.